Grammar & Writing Practice

Let's See Grammar Basic 1

Reflexive pronouns
反身代名詞

lick itself

彩圖初級英文文法 三版

written by Alex Rath Ph.D.

Counting an uncountable noun
不可數名詞
的計算

a box of chocolate

Uncountable nouns
不可數名詞

coffee

cheese

Expressions without "the"
不加the的情況

Countable nouns
可數名詞

have the breakfast

some apples

Basic 1 Contents

Part 3 Present Tenses 現在時態

Basic 2

Let's
See
Grammar

Basic 1

彩圖初級英文文法　三版

Answers to Small Exercises

p. 8   1. books   2. phones   3. tables

p. 10   1. candies   2. cities   3. halves   4. wives

p. 12   1. species   2. aircraft   3. bison   4. moose   5. trout/trouts

p. 16   1. an   2. a   3. the   4. the

p. 20   1. some   2. some

p. 22   1. Cars   2. Goats   3. The cars   4. The police / The police officers

p. 28   1. in/at church   2. in/at school

p. 32   1. my friend's   2. Joe's

p. 34   1. of the wall   2. of this school   3. of the boy   4. of the pig

p. 44   1. her   2. them   3. her   4. them

p. 46   1. their   2. His   3. yours

p. 48   1. some   2. any   3. any

p. 52   1. a little   2. a few   3. few   4. little

p. 54   1. one   2. ones

p. 76   1. they're   2. It is

p. 82   1. is raining   2. is reading   3. Are   4. studying   5. Is   6. swimming

p. 96   1. was   2. were   3. was   4. were

p. 116   1. am ordering   2. is playing   3. are   4. doing

p. 118   1. is going to clean   2. is going to visit

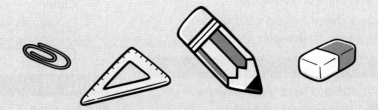

Answers to Practice Questions

Unit 1 p. 9

1 1. dogs 2. stars 3. dots 4. glasses
5. clocks 6. witches 7. faxes 8. bananas
9. fuzzes 10. crowns 11. mops 12. dishes
13. mugs 14. sponges 15. slashes 16. kites
17. rulers 18. branches 19. boxes 20. fans

2 1. trees 2. plants 3. hands 4. shirts
5. shoes 6. legs 7. paths

3 1. cats, months, parks, cups
2. mothers, erasers, jobs, stores
3. watches, lunches, foxes, bushes

Unit 2 p. 11

1 1. parties 2. leaves 3. photos 4. counties
5. armies 6. spies 7. wolves 8. tuxedos
9. shelves 10. pianos

2 1. jeans 2. sunglasses 3. ✗ 4. pants
5. ✗

3 1. ✓ 2. ✓
3. ✗ Be careful. Those knives are very sharp.
4. ✗ Leaves keep falling from the trees.
5. ✗ People say cats have nine lives.
6. ✗ I can't find the clothes I wore yesterday.
7. ✗ My father needs to wear glasses to read newspapers.
8. ✗ You can find three libraries in this city.

Unit 3 p. 13

1 1. bison 2. geese 3. aircraft/airplanes
4. goldfish/goldfishes 5. mice 6. oxen

2 1. C 2. B 3. C 4. A 5. C
6. A 7. B 8. A

Unit 4 p. 15

1 **Lydia bought:** a magazine, an ice cube tray, a lamp, an orange
Trent bought: a lightbulb, a fish, an umbrella

2 1. a cab 2. a glass of beer
3. a cup of coffee 4. an art museum
5. an opera 6. a café 7. an owl

Unit 5 p. 17

1 1. a, the 2. the, The, the, the, The, the
3. The, a 4. the, the, a 5. a, the

2 1. Ⓐ the channel Ⓑ a channel
2. Ⓐ a movie Ⓑ the movie
3. Ⓐ a sandwich Ⓑ the sandwich
4. Ⓐ a soda Ⓑ the soda

Unit 6 p. 19

1 可數：a comb, a hairdryer, a newspaper
不可數：shampoo, sugar, bread

2 1. is, ✗ 2. is, ✗ 3. is, a 4. are, the
5. is, a 6. is, a 7. is, an 8. is, a

3 1. hair 2. jewelry 3. makeup 4. OK
5. cosmetics 6. courage 7. OK

Unit 7 p. 21

1 1. two bottles of 2. two bars of
3. three jars of 4. a tube of 5. some
6. a bowl of 7. two cartons of
8. three sticks of 9. a piece of
10. a can of

2 1. Where can I buy some chocolate?
2. How much luggage do you have? / How many pieces of luggage do you have?
3. It's too quiet. I need some music.
4. How many bottles of perfume did you get?
5. Can you buy me two pieces of / some bread?
6. My brother wants to buy a piece of / some new furniture.

Unit 8 p. 23

1 1. Cats like boxes.
2. Cats like fish.
3. Cats like balls of yarn.
4. Cats don't like dogs.
5. Cats don't like showers.
6. Cats don't like vets.

2 1. Ⓐ Coffee Ⓑ The coffee
2. Ⓐ money Ⓑ the money
3. Ⓐ Rice Ⓑ The rice
4. Ⓐ attendance Ⓑ the class attendance

Unit 9 p. 25

1 1. the 2. ✗ 3. ✗ 4. ✗ 5. the 6. ✗ 7. ✗
8. the 9. ✗ 10. the 11. the 12. ✗ 13. the
14. the 15. the 16. ✗ 17. the 18. ✗
19. ✗ 20. ✗

2 1. "What are you reading?" "I'm reading **the China Post**."
2. Is **Mary** going to **Japan** with you?
3. **Jane** has a project due in **October**.
4. Why don't we see the latest movie in **the Miramar Cinema**?
5. Is the **Yellow River** the longest river in **China**?
6. Excuse me, how do I get to **Maple Street**?
7. Are you going to **the Evanston Public Library**?

Unit 10 p. 27

1 1. the radio 2. the theater 3. car
4. breakfast 5. the rain 6. TV

2 1. the 2. the 3. ✗ 4. the 5. ✗, ✗ 6. ✗

Unit 11 p. 29

1 1. the city 2. the violin 3. church
4. university 5. court
6. hospital（美式：the hospital）
2 1. the 2. ✗ 3. the, the, the 4. ✗ 5. ✗, ✗
6. the 7. the 8. ✗

Unit 12 p. 31

1 1. work 2. tennis 3. winter 4. math
5. home
2 1. ✗ 2. ✗, the 3. ✗, ✗ 4. ✗ 5. ✗ 6. ✗
3 The answers may vary.

Unit 13 p. 33

1 1. Catherine's key, Catherine's
2. Kiki's collar, Kiki's
3. Shakespeare's pen and ink, Shakespeare's
4. Tim Cook's briefcase, Tim Cook's
5. the wizard's magic wand, the wizard's
6. Kevin Durant's basketball, Kevin Durant's
2 1. student's, aunt's, Jeff's, tank's
2. Jennifer's, bottle's, lion's, kid's
3. Alice's, dish's, ox's, tax's

Unit 14 p. 35

1 1. the student's schoolbag
2. Jenny's iPad
3. Grandpa's newspaper
4. David's laptop
5. my sister's headphones
6. my brother's umbrella
7. the manager's cell phone
8. my mother's scarf
9. Liz's book
2 1. the light of the sun
2. the pile of trash
3. the keyboard of the computer
4. the speech of the president
5. the ninth symphony of Beethoven

Unit 15 Review Test p. 36

1 1. C 2. C 3. C 4. U 5. U 6. C 7. U 8. C
9. U 10. C 11. U 12. C 13. U 14. C 15. U
2 1. rats 2. dishes 3. watches 4. jelly candies
5. holidays 6. calves 7. Elves 8. teeth
9. fish 10. diaries
3 1. a carrot 2. a carrot 3. Carrots 4. a lion
5. the lion 6. Lions 7. sugar 8. the sugar
9. a banana 10. the banana 11. the keyboard
12. a keyboard 13. Music 14. the music
4 1. the suburbs 2. car 3. football 4. TV

5. home 6. dinner 7. bed 8. an Egyptian
9. the Nile River 10. Egyptians 11. Brazil
12. the Amazon River 13. new sources
14. scientists 15. tourists
5 1. a camera 2. potatoes 3. hair 4. a box
5. a loaf 6. lots of snow 7. is 8. are 9. Is
6 1. Ⓐ Ned's suitcase
Ⓑ the suitcase of Ned
2. Ⓐ my father's jacket
Ⓑ the jacket of my father
3. Ⓐ my sister's colored pencils
Ⓑ the colored pencils of my sister
4. Ⓐ ✗
Ⓑ the corner of the bathroom
5. Ⓐ Edward's brother
Ⓑ the brother of Edward
6. Ⓐ ✗
Ⓑ the end of the vacation
7 1. **a bottle of:** soy sauce, wine, lotion
2. **a jar of:** pickles, peanut butter, strawberry jam
3. **a piece of:** luggage, cheese, jewelry
4. **a can of:** tuna, shaving cream, soda
5. **a bowl of:** grapes, salad, rice
6. **a tube of:** watercolor, cleansing foam, ointment
7. **a pot of:** tea, coffee, soup
8. **a packet of:** potato chips, ketchup, cookies
8 （例子僅供參考）
1. ✓ : the Shed Aquarium, the Field Museum
2. ✓ : the Hilton Hotel, the Metro Café
3. ✗ : Monday, Tuesday
4. ✓ : the New Wave Cinema, the Varsity Multiplex
5. ✓ : the Pacific Ocean, the Aegean Sea
6. ✗ : Sri Lanka, Europe
7. ✓ : Jennifer Lawrence, Justin Timberlake
8. ✗ : Madison Avenue, Hollywood Boulevard
9. ✗ : March, May
10. ✗ : Spaniards, Japanese
11. ✓ : the Concord River, the River Thames
12. ✗ : Tuxedo Junction, Long Island City

Unit 16 p. 43

1 1. I 2. You 3. She 4. It 5. It 6. We
7. They 8. She 9. He
2 1. They 2. He 3. She 4. He 5. She
6. He 7. It 8. We

Unit 17 p. 45

1 1. I like him. / I don't like him.
2. I like it. / I don't like it.

3. I like it. / I don't like it.
4. I like it. / I don't like it.
5. I like them. / I don't like them.
6. I like her. / I don't like her.

2 1. us 2. us 3. him 4. me 5. him 6. her
   7. them 8. it 9. him 10. us 11. him 12. us

Unit 18   p. 47

1 1. My 2. our 3. his 4. her 5. their
   6. their 7. Our 8. his, her, their

2 1. your, hers 2. my, your 3. your, mine
   4. its 5. Yours

Unit 19   p. 49

1 1. There aren't any eggs.
   2. There's some meat.
   3. There isn't any ice.
   4. There are some bottled waters.
   5. There are some vegetables.
   6. There isn't any milk.

2 1. There's no space.
   2. We haven't got any newspapers.
   3. She's got no money.
   4. There aren't any boxes.
   5. I haven't got any blank disks.
   6. He doesn't have any bonus points.

3 1. some 2. some 3. any 4. some
   5. no 6. any

Unit 20   p. 51

1 1. How many televisions do you want?
   2. How many cell phone batteries do you want?
   3. How many cameras do you want?
   4. How much detergent do you want?
   5. How many lightbulbs do you want?
   6. How many air conditioners do you want?
   7. How many water filters do you want?

2 1. too much 2. too much 3. too many
   4. too many 5. too much 6. too much
   7. enough

Unit 21   p. 53

1 （此題答案可有變化，僅供參考）
   1. There are a lot of bananas.
   2. There are many books.
   3. There are a lot of masks.
   4. There isn't much beer.
   5. There are a few sandwiches.
   6. There are a lot of gift boxes.
   7. There are many candles.
   8. There are a few passion fruits.

2 1. much 2. a few 3. Little / A little
   4. a lot of 5. many / a lot of 6. a little

Unit 22   p. 55

1 1. one, one, one 2. one, one, one
   3. ones, ones, one, ones, one

Unit 23   p. 57

1 1. someone, anyone, anyone
   2. anyone, someone
   3. someone, someone, someone
   4. anyone, anyone, someone, anyone
   5. Someone, anyone

2 1. go 2. to talk 3. Someone 4. someone
   5. anyone 6. to keep 7. someone

Unit 24   p. 59

1 1. anything to eat 2. anything to drink
   3. anywhere to go 4. something to do

2 1. anything, anything 2. to hide
   3. something 4. something
   5. anywhere 6. to read
   7. anywhere, anything, to do

Unit 25   p. 61

1 1. There is nobody at the office.
   2. There is no one leaving today.
   3. There is nothing to feed the fish.
   4. There is nowhere to buy envelops around here.
   5. There isn't anybody here who can speak Japanese.
   6. There isn't anyone that can translate your letter.
   7. There isn't anything that will change the manager's mind.
   8. There isn't anywhere we can go to get out of the rain.

2 1. I have nowhere to go. / I don't have anywhere to go.
   2. No one believed me.
   3. Everything is ready. Let's go.
   4. There is nothing to eat.
   5. I never want to hurt anybody.
   6. Everyone in this room will vote for me.
   7. Did you see my glasses? I can't find it anywhere.
   8. Anyone who doesn't support this idea please raise your hand.

Unit 26   p. 63

1 1. This 2. These 3. this 4. That 5. Those
   6. these

2 1. this   2. that   3. those   4. these
5. that   6. this   7. Those   8. these
9. That   10. those

Unit 27 p. 65

1 1. myself   2. yourself   3. itself   4. himself
5. herself   6. yourself   7. ourselves
8. themselves

2 1. each other   2. themselves   3. themselves

Unit 28 Review Test p. 66

1 1. my   2. I   3. mine   4. me   5. My   6. I
7. me   8. mine

2 1. My, your   2. I, Our   3. her   4. my
5. he, her   6. I, mine, you, mine
7. their, ours   8. it   9. It, them
10. Their, They, it   11. your, It, mine

3 1. wine / green peppers
2. bread / cookies   3. sugar   4. toothpaste
5. candy   6. grapes   7. fish / goats
8. medicine   9. chocolate cakes / fruit tarts
10. soup / soda   11. garlic   12. notebooks

4 1. We have any rice. **some**
2. Are there any spoons in the drawer? **OK**
3. There isn't some orange juice in the refrigerator. **any**
4. Are there any cookies in the box? **OK**
5. Could I have any coffee, please? **some**
6. Would you like some ham? **OK**
7. We have lots of fruit. Would you like any? **some**
8. I already had some fruit at home. I don't need some now. **any**
9. There aren't some newspapers. **any**
10. There are any magazines. **some**

5 1. Who are these boxes for, the **ones** you are carrying?
2. Do you like the red socks or the yellow **ones**?
3. My cubicle is the **one** next to the manager's office.
4. I like the pink hat. Which **one** do you like?
5. Our tennis balls are the **ones** stored over there.

6 1. B   2. B   3. B   4. A   5. B
6. A   7. A   8. A   9. A   10. B

7 1. everywhere   2. nowhere   3. anywhere
4. somewhere   5. no one   6. anyone
7. Someone   8. Everyone   9. something
10. anything   11. nothing   12. everything
13. everybody   14. anybody   15. somebody
16. nobody

8 1. someone   2. No one   3. anyone

4. Everyone   5. No one   6. somewhere
7. anywhere   8. nowhere   9. everywhere
10. somewhere   11. something   12. anything
13. nothing   14. everything

9 1. A   2. A   3. C   4. B   5. B   6. A

10 1. My brother made himself sick by eating too much ice cream. **OK**
2. My sister made himself sick by eating two big pizzas. **herself**
3. The dog is scratching itself. **OK**
4. I jog every morning by me. **myself**
5. You have only yourself to blame. **OK**
6. We would have gone there us but we didn't have time. **ourselves**
7. He can't possibly lift that sofa all by himself. **OK**
8. Do you want to finish this project by yourself or do you need help? **OK**
9. I helped him. He helped me. We helped ourselves. **each other**
10. Don't fight about it. You two need to talk to each other if you are going to solve this problem. **OK**

11 1. a little   2. a few   3. enough   4. a lot of
5. enough   6. a lot   7. little   8. Few
9. enough   10. many   11. a few   12. a lot of
13. too many   14. enough

Unit 29 p. 75

1 1. is   2. am   3. is   4. is   5. is   6. is   7. are
8. are   9. am   10. is   11. are   12. are
13. is   14. are

2 (此題答案可能不同，僅供參考)
1. am   2. am   3. am not   4. is   5. are
6. isn't   7. are   8. are

3 1. Karl is Canadian. He is a violinist.
2. Dominique is Italian. He is a chef.
3. Hiroko is Japanese. She is a drummer.
4. Lino is French. He is a businessman.
5. Jane is Chinese. She is a singer.
6. Mike is American. He is a policeman.

Unit 30 p. 77

1 1. There isn't   2. There are   3. There isn't
4. There are   5. There is   6. There is
7. There is   8. There isn't   9. There isn't
10. There are   11. There isn't   12. There are
13. There aren't   14. There is   15. There isn't
16. There are

2 (此題答案可能不同，僅供參考)
1. is, It is   2. isn't, it   3. is, It is
4. are, They are   5. are, They are   6. is, It is

Unit 31
p. 79

1 1. She's got a hamster.　2. She's got a parrot.
3. They've got a cat.　4. He's got a dog.
5. She's got a snake.　6. He's got a pig.

2 1. Has your family got a cottage on Lake Michigan?
2. Have you got your own room?
3. Have you got your own closet?
4. How many cups have you got?
5. How many TVs has your family got?
6. How many cars has your brother got?

Unit 32
p. 81

1 1. eats　2. drinks　3. walks　4. runs
5. paints　6. buries　7. watches
8. carries　9. unboxes　10. crunches
11. tries　12. chases　13. cuts　14. goes
15. fixes　16. teaches

2 **Bobby:** I **cook** simple food every day. I usually **heat** food in the microwave oven. I often **make** sandwiches. I sometimes **pour** hot water on fast noodles. However, I **don't wash** dishes.
Jenny: I usually **get up** at 6:00 in the morning. I **eat** breakfast at 6:30. I **leave** my house at 7:00. I **walk** to the bus stop. I **take** the 7:15 bus. I always **get** to work at 8:00. I **have** lunch at 12:30. I **leave** work at 5:30. I **take** the bus home. I **arrive** at my home about 6:30. I **eat** dinner at 7:00. I often **fall asleep** after the 11:00 news ends.

3 1. cuts　2. tightens　3. makes　4. moves
5. pounds　6. pushes

Unit 33
p. 83

1 1. talking　2. caring　3. staying　4. sleeping
5. jogging　6. eating　7. making　8. robbing
9. advising　10. dying　11. spitting
12. staring　13. waiting　14. clipping
15. swimming　16. crying　17. lying
18. planning　19. throwing　20. speaking

2 1. is walking　2. is buying　3. is shining
4. is playing　5. are picnicking　6. is lying
7. are running　8. is eating　9. is sitting

Unit 34
p. 85

1 1. driving　2. leaves　3. designs　4. ends
5. drinks　6. is thinking　7. goes　8. wishes

2 1. **Q:** Do you often listen to music?
A: Yes, I do. I often listen to music.
2. **Q:** Are you watching TV at this moment?
A: Yes, I am. I'm watching TV at this moment. / No, I'm not. I'm not watching TV at this moment.

3. **Q:** Is it hot now?
A: Yes, it is. It is hot now. / No, it isn't. It isn't hot now.
4. **Q:** Is it often hot this time of year?
A: Yes, it is. It is often hot this time of year. / No, it isn't. It isn't often hot this time of year.
5. **Q:** Do you drink coffee every day?
A: Yes, I do. I drink coffee every day. / No, I don't. I don't drink coffee every day.
6. **Q:** Are you drinking tea right now?
A: Yes, I am. I'm drinking tea right now. / No, I'm not. I'm not drinking tea right now.

Unit 35
p. 87

1 1. am eating, hate　2. is eating, likes
3. loves　4. likes　5. are making, know
6. Do, mean　7. seem, are, doing
8. Are, going, Do, need
9. is carrying, belongs　10. Do, understand
11. remembers

2 1. I ~~am owning~~ my own house.　**own**
2. This book belongs to Mary.　**OK**
3. Mother ~~is believing~~ your story.　**believes**
4. I often forget names.　**OK**
5. I am having a snack.　**OK**
6. The man ~~is recognizing~~ you.　**recognized**
7. The story ~~is needing~~ an ending.　**needs**
8. You ~~are seeming~~ a little uncomfortable. **seem**
9. Are you feeling sick?　**OK**
10. Do you ~~have got~~ a swimsuit?　**have**

Unit 36 Review Test
p. 88

1 1. changes, changing　2. visits, visiting
3. turns, turning　4. jogs, jogging
5. mixes, mixing　6. cries, crying
7. has, having　8. cuts, cutting
9. fights, fighting　10. feels, feeling
11. ties, tying　12. applies, applying
13. jumps, jumping　14. enjoys, enjoying
15. steals, stealing　16. swims, swimming
17. sends, sending　18. tastes, tasting
19. finishes, finishing　20. studies, studying

2 1. **Q:** What is your favorite TV show?
A: The Simpsons.（参考答案）
2. **Q:** What is your favorite movie?
A: The Godfather.（参考答案）
3. **Q:** Who is your favorite actor?
A: Johnny Depp.（参考答案）
4. **Q:** Who is your favorite actress?
A: Nicole Kidman.（参考答案）
5. **Q:** What is your favorite food?

A: Hamburgers.（參考答案）

6. Q: What is your favorite juice?
   A: Orange juice.（參考答案）

7. Q: Who are your parents?
   A: Mike and Jennifer.（參考答案）

8. Q: Who are your brothers and sisters?
   A: James, David, and Alice.（參考答案）

3 1. Q: **Is** Seoul in Vietnam?
      A: **No, Seoul is in Korea.**

   2. Q: **Are** Thailand and Vietnam in East Asia?
      A: **No, they are in Southeast Asia.**

   3. Q: **Is** Hong Kong in Japan?
      A: **No, Hong Kong is in China.**

   4. Q: **Are** Beijing and Shanghai in China?
      A: **Yes, they are in China.**

   5. Q: **Is** Osaka in Taiwan?
      A: **No, Osaka is in Japan.**

   6. Q: **Are** Tokyo, Osaka, and Kyoto in Japan?
      A: **Yes, they are in Japan.**

4 1. Q: **Are there** any men's shoe stores?
      A: **Yes, there are.**

   2. Q: **Is there** a wig store?
      A: **No, there isn't.**

   3. Q: **Is there** a computer store?
      A: **No, there isn't.**

   4. Q: **Are there** two bookstores?
      A: **No, there aren't.**

   5. Q: **Are there** any women's clothing stores?
      A: **Yes, there is (one).**

   6. Q: **Are there** any women's shoe stores?
      A: **Yes, there is (one).**

   7. Q: **Are there** three music stores?
      A: **No, there aren't.**

   8. Q: **Is there** a jewelry store?
      A: **Yes, there is.**

5 1. is   2. am   3. have   4. are   5. has
   6. are   7. am   8. are   9. are   10. am

6 1. Q: **Are** you a university student?
      A: Yes, I am. / No, I'm not.

   2. Q: **Are** you a big reader?
      A: Yes, I am. / No, I'm not.

   3. Q: **Is** your birthday coming soon?
      A: Yes, it is. / No, it isn't.

   4. Q: **Is** your favorite holiday Chinese New Year?
      A: Yes, it is. / No, it isn't.

7 （參考答案）
   · There is an alarm clock on the dresser.
   · There are two pillows on the bed.
   · There is a chair in the room.
   · There is a candle on the dresser.
   · There is a pen and a bottle of ink on the dresser.
   · There are some books on the shelf.
   · There is a light hanging from the ceiling.

· There is a dresser in the room.
· There is a bed in the room.

8 1. Do   2. work   3. don't   4. work   5. Does
   6. work   7. works   8. Does   9. work
   10. doesn't   11. work   12. works

9 1. Q: Do you watch many movies?
      A: Yes, I do. I watch many movies. / No, I don't. I don't watch many movies.

   2. Q: Does your mother work?
      A: Yes, she does. She works. / No, she doesn't. She doesn't work.

   3. Q: Does your father drive a car to work?
      A: Yes, he does. He drives a car to work. / No, he doesn't. He doesn't drive a car to work.

   4. Q: Does your family have a big house?
      A: Yes, we do. My family has a big house. / We have a big house. / No, we don't. We don't have a big house. / My family doesn't have a big house.

   5. Q: Do your neighbors have children?
      A: Yes, they do. They have children. / No, they don't. They don't have children.

   6. Q: Do you have a university degree?
      A: Yes, I do. I have a university degree. / No, I don't. I don't have a university degree.

10 1. do you like to be called
    2. do you come from
    3. do you go to the café
    4. do you drink at the café
    5. do you go home
    6. do you go home
    7. do you have to be at school

11 1. Peter has got a good car.   2. ✗
    3. Wendy has got a brother and a sister.
    4. The Hamiltons have got two cars.
    5. Ken has got a lot of good ideas.
    6. ✗   7. I have got the answer sheet.

12 1. is fixing   2. is delivering
    3. is changing   4. is talking   5. are using
    6. are working

13 1. I am going   2. stop   3. He often has
    4. is having   5. wants   6. is having
    7. I'm thinking   8. I have got
    9. I don't believe   10. I can hear

14 1. We aren't tired. Are we tired?
    2. You aren't rich. Are you rich?
    3. There isn't a message for Jim. Is there a message for Jim?
    4. It isn't a surprise. Is it a surprise?
    5. They haven't got tickets. Have they got tickets?
    6. You haven't got electric power. Have you got electric power?

7. She doesn't work out at the gym.
   Does she work out at the gym?
8. He doesn't usually drink a fitness shake for breakfast.
   Does he usually drink a fitness shake for breakfast?
9. We aren't playing baseball this weekend.
   Are we playing baseball this weekend?
10. He doesn't realize this is the end of the vacation.
    Does he realize this is the end of the vacation?

Unit 37
p. 97

1 1. was, is   2. was , is   3. is, was   4. is, was
   5. is, was   6. was, is   7. were, are
   8. were, are   9. are, were   10. were, are
   11. were, are   12. were, are
2 1. **Were** you busy yesterday?
   Yes, I was. I was very busy yesterday. / No, I wasn't. I wasn't very busy yesterday.
2. **Were** you at school yesterday morning?
   Yes, I was. I was at school yesterday morning. / No, I wasn't. I wasn't at school yesterday morning.
3. **Was** yesterday the busiest day of the week?
   Yes, it was. It was the busiest day of the week. / No, it wasn't. It wasn't the busiest day of the week.
4. **Was** your father in the office last night?
   Yes, he was. He was in the office last night. / No, he wasn't. he wasn't in the office last night.
5. **Were** you at your friend's house last Saturday?
   Yes, I was. I was at my friend's house last Saturday. / No, I wasn't. I wasn't at my friend's house last Saturday.
6. **Was** your mother at home at 8 o'clock yesterday morning?
   Yes, she was. She was at home at 8 o'clock yesterday morning. / No, she wasn't. She wasn't at home at 8 o'clock yesterday morning.
7. **Were** you in bed at 11 o'clock last night?
   Yes, I was. I was in bed at 11 o'clock last night. / No, I wasn't. I wasn't in bed at 11 o'clock last night.
8. **Were** you at the bookstore at 6 o'clock yesterday evening?
   Yes, I was. I was at the bookstore at 6 o'clock yesterday evening. / No, I wasn't. I wasn't at the bookstore at 6 o'clock yesterday evening.

Unit 38
p. 99

1 1. walked   2. ran   3. coughed   4. wrote
   5. ate   6. dropped   7. asked   8. picked
   9. showed   10. drank   11. waited
   12. typed   13. married   14. flied   15. went
   16. used   17. joined   18. played   19. looked
   20. liked   21. sent   22. jogged
2 1. counted   2. attended   3. received
   4. used   5. checked   6. put

Unit 39
p. 101

1 1. Did, had, didn't have   2. Did, have, did
   3. did, have, had
2 1. **Q:** Did you see your friends last night?
   A: Yes, I did. I saw my friends last night. / No, I didn't. I didn't see my friends last night.
2. **Q:** Did you go to a movie last weekend?
   A: Yes, I did. I went to a movie last weekend. / No, I didn't. I didn't go to a movie last weekend.
3. **Q:** Did you play basketball yesterday?
   A: Yes, I did. I played basketball yesterday. / No, I didn't. I didn't play basketball yesterday.
4. **Q:** Did you graduate from university last year?
   A: Yes, I did. I graduated from university last year. / No, I didn't. I didn't graduate from university last year.
5. **Q:** Did you move out of your parents' house last month?
   A: Yes, I did. I moved out of my parents' house last month. / No, I didn't. I didn't move out of my parents' house last month.
3 1. was   2. saw   3. was   4. pondered
   5. succeeded

Unit 40
p. 103

1 1. were decorating   2. was hanging
   3. was draping   4. was arranging
   5. was putting   6. was unpacking
   7. was putting
2 1. **Q: What was she doing** when the phone rang?
   A: She was sleeping soundly.
2. **Q: What was he doing** while walking?
   A: He was talking on the phone.
3. **Q: What was he doing** while watching TV during breakfast?
   A: He was drinking coffee.

10

Unit 41 p. 105

1 1. eaten 2. seen 3. written 4. gone
5. loved 6. come 7. fought 8. read
9. got/gotten 10. left 11. brought 12. lent
13. cost 14. lost 15. hit 16. paid
17. found 18. taken 19. rung 20. spoken

2 1. has eaten 2. has taught 3. has arrived
4. has won 5. has stolen 6. has written

3　　Clive grew up in the country. He moved
to the city in 2010. He **has lived** there since
then.
　　He **has worked** in an Italian restaurant
for a year and half. He met his wife in the
restaurant. They got married last month, and
she moved in to his apartment. They **have
become** a happy couple, but they **haven't
had** a baby yet.

Unit 42 p. 107

1 1. have been, since 2. have built, for
3. for 4. have piloted 5. have worked, for
6. have dreamed 7. have wondered
8. Since, have started

2 1. Q: Have you ever eaten a worm?
A: Yes, I have. I have eaten a worm. / No, I
haven't. I haven't eaten a worm.
2. Q: Have you ever been to Japan?
A: Yes, I have. I have been to Japan./ No, I
haven't. I haven't been to Japan.
3. Q: Have you ever swum in the ocean?
A: Yes, I have. I have swum in the ocean.
/ No, I haven't. I haven't swum in the
ocean.
4. Q: Have you ever cheated on an exam?
A: Yes, I have. I have cheated on an exam.
/ No, I haven't. I haven't / I have never
cheated on an exam.

Unit 43 p. 109

1 1. has loved 2. has been 3. stayed
4. went surfing 5. liked 6. discovered
7. rented 8. learned 9. visited
10. has enjoyed 11. has fished 12. visited
13. has gone 14. has talked

2 1. has he been 2. was 3. has he been
4. Did he go 5. Did he stay
6. Has he visited 7. When was

Unit 44 Review Test p. 110

1 1. drove, driven 2. went, gone 3. ate, eaten
4. wrote, written 5. thought, thought
6. kept, kept 7. drank, drunk 8. slept, slept
9. made, made 10. stood, stood

11. bought, bought 12. sang, sung
13. did, done 14. hid, hid/hidden
15. fell, fallen 16. said, said 17. gave, given
18. sat, sat 19. shot, shot 20. taught, taught

2 1. I **sailed** on a friend's boat last weekend.
→ **I didn't sail on a friend's boat last
weekend.**
→ **Did I sail on a friend's boat last
weekend?**
2. I **saw** the seals on the rocks.
→ **I didn't see the seals on the rocks.**
→ **Did I see the seals on the rocks?**
3. We **fed** the seagulls.
→ **We didn't feed the seagulls.**
→ **Did we feed the seagulls?**
4. The seagull **liked** the bread we threw to it.
→ **The seagull didn't like the bread we
threw to it.**
→ **Did the seagull like the bread we threw
to it?**
5. We **fished** for our dinner.
→ **We didn't fish for our dinner.**
→ **Did we fish for our dinner?**
6. My friend **cooked** our dinner in the galley
of the boat.
→ **My friend didn't cook our dinner in the
galley of the boat.**
→ **Did my friend cook our dinner in the
galley of the boat?**
7. We **ate** on deck.
→ **We didn't eat on deck.**
→ **Did we eat on deck?**
8. We **passed** the time chatting and watching
the water.
→ **We didn't pass the time chatting and
watching the water.**
→ **Did we pass the time chatting and
watching the water?**

3 1. called, ordered, played, brushed
2. fixed, hiked, walked, marched
3. started, landed, carted, handed

4 Catherine **got** up at 5:00. She **took** a shower.
Then she **made** a cup of strong black coffee.
She **sat** at her computer and **checked** her
email. She **answered** her email and **worked**
on her computer until 7:30. At 7:30, she **ate**
a light breakfast. After breakfast, she **went**
to work. She **walked** to work. She **bought** a
cup of coffee and a newspaper on her way to
work. She **arrived** promptly at 8:30 and **was**
ready to start her day at the office.

5 1. was snowing, went 2. fell, had
3. were walking, saw 4. saw, said
5. fell 6. broke, fell 7. was feeding, heard
8. woke, realized 9. started

6 1. **Q:** Have they picked up the flyers yet?
   A: Yes, they have. They have already picked up the flyers.
2. **Q:** Have they put out order pads yet?
   A: Yes, they have. They have already put out order pads.
3. **Q:** Have they gotten pens with their company logo yet?
   A: No, they haven't. They haven't gotten pens with their company logo yet.
4. **Q:** Have they set up the computer yet?
   A: No, they haven't. They haven't set up the computer yet.
5. **Q:** Have they arranged flowers yet?
   A: Yes, they have. They have already arranged flowers.
6. **Q:** Have they unpacked boxes yet?
   A: No, they haven't. They haven't unpacked boxes yet.

7 （答案略）

8 1. was   2. was, was   3. had
   4. bought   5. slept   6. have gone
   7. kept, died   8. registered
   9. Have, finished, haven't finished
   10. was cooking   11. did

9 1. B   2. B   3. B   4. A   5. A   6. A   7. A
   8. A   9. B

Unit 45 p. 117

1 1. Who **is going** on vacation?
   → **Mark and Sharon are going on vacation.**
2. When **are** Mark and Sharon **going** on vacation?
   → **They are going on vacation on May 18ᵗʰ.**
3. Where **are** they **departing** from?
   → **They are departing from Linz.**
4. Where **are** they **flying** to?
   → **They are flying to Budapest.**
5. What time **are** they **departing**?
   → **They are departing at 15:30.**
6. What time **are** they **arriving** at their destination?
   → **They are arriving at their destination at 17:30.**
7. What airline **are** they **taking**?
   → **They are taking Aeroflot Airlines.**
8. What flight **are** they **taking**?
   → **They are taking Flight 345.**

Unit 46 p. 119

1 1. No, he isn't. He is going to use a laptop.
2. Yes, she is. She's going to buy some vegetables.

3. Yes, she is. She's going to take a nap with her teddy bear.
4. No, they aren't. They're going to drink some orange juice.
5. No, they aren't. They are going to buy some books.
6. No, she isn't. She's going to give the customers a key.

2 1. I'm going to eat at a restaurant. / I'm not going to eat at a restaurant.
2. I'm going to watch a baseball game. / I'm not going to watch a baseball game.
3. I'm going to read a book. / I'm not going to read a book.
4. I'm going to play video games. / I'm not going to play video games.
5. I'm going to write an email. / I'm not going to write an email.

Unit 47 p. 121

1 1. Will scientists clone humans in 50 years?
   Scientists will clone humans in 50 years.
   Scientists won't clone humans in 50 years.
2. Will robots become family members in 80 years?
   Robots will become family members in 80 years.
   Robots won't become family members in 80 years.
3. Will doctors insert memory chips behind our ears?
   Doctors will insert memory chips behind our ears.
   Doctors won't insert memory chips behind our ears.
4. Will police officers scan our brains for criminal thoughts?
   Police officers will scan our brains for criminal thoughts.
   Police officers won't scan our brains for criminal thoughts.

2 1. I think I'll live in another country.
   Perhaps I'll live in another country.
   I doubt I'll live in another country.
2. I think my sister will learn how to drive.
   Perhaps my sister will learn how to drive.
   I doubt my sister will learn how to drive.
3. I think Jerry will marry somebody from another country.
   Perhaps Jerry will marry somebody from another country.
   I doubt Jerry will marry somebody from another country.
4. I don't think Tammy will go abroad again.
   Perhaps Tammy will not go abroad again.
   I doubt Tammy will go abroad again.

Unit 48
p. 123

1 1. Are you going to the bookstore tomorrow?
  2. Janet is going to help Cindy move in to her new house.
  3. Are you playing baseball this Saturday?
  4. He will cook dinner at 5:30.
  5. She will fall into the water.
  6. I'm going to give him a call tonight.
  7. When are you going to get up tomorrow morning?
  8. I'm driving to Costco this afternoon.
2 1. is leaving   2. will melt   3. will quit
  4. am going to quit   5. will eat   6. is having
  7. am going to find, am going to make
  8. will rain

Unit 49 Review Test
p. 124

1 1. I **am going** out for lunch tomorrow.
  → **I am not going out for lunch tomorrow.**
  → **Am I going out for lunch tomorrow?**
  2. I **am planning** a birthday party for my grandmother.
  → **I'm not planning a birthday party for my grandmother.**
  → **Am I planning a birthday party for my grandmother?**
  3. She **is going** to take the dog for a walk after dinner.
  → **She isn't going to take the dog for a walk after dinner.**
  → **Is she going to take the dog for a walk after dinner?**
  4. Mike **is planning** to watch a baseball game later tonight.
  → **Mike isn't planning to watch a baseball game later tonight.**
  → **Is Mike planning to watch a baseball game later tonight?**
  5. Dr. Johnson **is meeting** a patient at the clinic on Saturday.
  → **Dr. Johnson isn't meeting a patient at the clinic on Saturday.**
  → **Is Dr. Johnson meeting a patient at the clinic on Saturday?**
  6. Jack and Kim **are applying** for admission to a technical college.
  → **Jack and Kim aren't applying for admission to a technical college.**
  → **Are Jack and Kim applying for admission to a technical college?**
  7. I **am thinking** about having two kids after I get married.
  → **I'm not thinking about having two kids after I get married.**
  → **Am I thinking about having two kids after I get married?**

  8. Josh **is playing** basketball this weekend.
  → **Josh isn't playing basketball this weekend.**
  → **Is Josh playing basketball this weekend?**
  9. My little brother **is planning** to sleep late on Sunday morning.
  → **My little brother isn't planning to sleep late on Sunday morning.**
  → **Is my little brother planning to sleep late on Sunday morning?**
  10. Father and I **are working** out at the gym on Sunday.
  → **Father and I aren't working out at the gym on Sunday.**
  → **Are Father and I working out at the gym on Sunday?**
2 1. F   2. C   3. C   4. C   5. C   6. F   7. F   8. C
3 1. What **are** you **going to do** tomorrow night?
  I'm going to do some shopping tomorrow night.
  2. When **are** you **going to leave**?
  I'm going to leave at 9 a.m.
  3. **Is** he **going to call** her later?
  Yes, he is going to call her later.
  4. What **are** you **going to say** when you see him?
  I'm going to tell him the truth.
  5. **Are** they **going to study** British Literature in college?
  No, they are going to study Chinese Literature in college.
  6. **Is** your family **going to have** a vacation in Hawaii?
  No, my family is going to have a vacation in Guam.
4 1. I think I'll take a nap.
  2. I think I'll turn on a light.
  3. I think I'll check my voicemail.
  4. I think I'll eat them right away.
  5. I think I'll pay it at 7-Eleven.
  6. I think I'll buy him a gift.
  7. I think I'll visit her in the hospital.
  8. I think I'll bring my umbrella.
5 1. ✓   2. ✗   I think it'll rain soon.   3. ✓
  4. ✗ I'm sure you won't get called next week.
  5. ✓   6. ✗ Is Laura going to work?   7. ✓
  8. ✗ In the year 2100, people will live on the moon.
  9. ✗ What are you doing next week?
6 1. A   2. A   3. A   4. A

13

7 1. I won't be watching the game on Saturday afternoon.
Will I be watching the game on Saturday afternoon?

2. You aren't going to visit Grandma Moses tomorrow.
Are you going to visit Grandma Moses tomorrow?

3. She isn't planning to be on vacation next week.
Is she planning to be on vacation next week?

4. We aren't going to take a trip to New Zealand next month.
Are we going to take a trip to New Zealand next month?

5. He won't send the tax forms soon.
Will he send the tax forms soon?

6. It won't be cold all next week.
Will it be cold all next week?

8 1. A 2. A 3. B 4. C 5. A 6. B 7. B
8. A 9. C 10. A 11. C 12. B

Progress Test

Part 1	p. 130

1 1. C 2. C 3. C 4. C 5. U 6. C 7. U 8. U
9. U 10. C 11. C 12. U 13. U 14. C 15. C
16. U 17. U 18. U 19. U 20. U

2 1. giraffes 2. dishes 3. oxen 4. lives
5. ducks 6. churches 7. sizes 8. erasers
9. geese 10. televisions 11. pencils
12. oases 13. cherries 14. species
15. libraries 16. data 17. sheep 18. fairies
19. deer 20. witches

3 1. a 2. the 3. a 4. an 5. a 6. An 7. a
8. An, the 9. an 10. the 11. an 12. The
13. a 14. the 15. an 16. a 17. the
18. the, a

4 1. bottles 2. box 3. tube 4. cups 5. carton
6. jar 7. can 8. bowl 9. glass 10. head

5 1. traffic 2. furniture 3. scissors 4. milk
5. tea 6. coffee

6 1. ✗ 2. the 3. the 4. ✗ 5. the 6. The
7. ✗ 8. ✗ 9. the 10. the, the 11. ✗, ✗
12. ✗ 13. the 14. ✗, ✗

7 1. ✗ Calvin is a cool little kid.
2. ✗ Our vacation starts on Friday, January 20th.
3. ✓
4. ✗ The nearest airport is in Canberra.
5. ✗ The Museum of Modern Art in New York is 50 years old.

6. ✗ The Great Wall of China is pretty amazing.

8 1. Jane's hat 2. my grandparents' house
3. the side of the road
4. Beethoven's Fifth Symphony
5. the price tags of the products
6. the ruins of ancient civilizations

9 1. ✓ 2. ✓
3. ✗ Are you watching TV or doing homework?
4. ✓
5. ✗ Helen has decided to learn the piano.
6. ✗ The closest star to us is the Sun.

Part 2	p. 133

1 1. I 2. you 3. You 4. We 5. he 6. They
7. she 8. it

2 1. me 2. you 3. him 4. her 5. it 6. us
7. You 8. them 9. ours 10. my 11. yours
12. yours 13. yours 14. mine 15. hers

3 1. my 2. our 3. its 4. their 5. her 6. his
7. your

4 1. some 2. any 3. any 4. some 5. any
6. any 7. some 8. some 9. any 10. any
11. some 12. some 13. any 14. any 15. any
16. some 17. any 18. any 19. some
20. some 21. any 22. some 23. any

5 1. any 2. some 3. no 4. any 5. some
6. some 7. No 8. some 9. Any 10. some

6 1. A 2. C 3. B 4. C 5. A 6. B

7 1. little 2. a few 3. little 4. A little
5. a few 6. a few 7. a few 8. a little

8 1. one, a glass of juice 2. ones, ties
3. one, pair of shoes 4. one, jacket

9 1. Everybody / Everyone 2. anybody / anyone
3. anything 4. somebody / someone
5. something 6. nowhere
7. Nobody / No one 8. anywhere 9. nothing

10 1. that 2. this 3. these 4. that 5. those

11 1. himself 2. herself 3. ourselves
4. themselves 5. myself 6. yourself

Part 3	p. 136

1 1. am 2. is 3. is 4. am 5. am 6. are
7. is 8. are 9. is 10. am 11. is

2 1. Is there 2. There are 3. It is 4. Are there
5. it is 6. there is

3 1. have got 2. haven't got
3. Have, got, have 4. have got, haven't got

4 1. work 2. take 3. commutes 4. do, get
5. don't drive, don't know 6. Do, go
7. takes

5 1. are, doing　2. is ringing　3. am, cooking
　4. is looking　5. Are, working
　6. am planning

6 1. B　2. B　3. C　4. C　5. A　6. C　7. B
　8. B　9. A

7 1. ✗ I want something to eat.
　2. ✗ I love that dress you are wearing.
　3. ✓
　4. ✗ I think you are right about Jim.
　5. ✓
　6. ✗ I saw some new shopping bags in your
　　closet.

Part 4　　　　　　　　　　　p. 138

1 1. Were, were　2. Was, wasn't　3. Was, was
　4. Were, weren't

2 1. Did　2. go　3. met　4. happened　5. ate
　6. talked　7. did　8. do　9. stayed
　10. behaved　11. meant　12. was

3 1. was standing　2. was sitting　3. pulled up
　4. grabbed　5. noticed
　6. was looking / looked　7. started
　8. opened　9. began　10. discovered

4 1. has been　2. Have, attended　3. has had
　4. has left　5. has been

5 1. opened　2. have had　3. Have you been
　4. Did you go

Part 5　　　　　　　　　　　p. 139

1 1. Are　2. seeing　3. am seeing　4. am going
　5. Are　6. coming　7. am meeting　8. Are
　9. taking　10. am visiting

2 1. am going to sleep　2. are, going to visit
　3. Are, going to quit　4. are, going to move
　5. Are, going to live

3 1. will wonder　2. won't date　3. will send
　4. will screen　5. won't respond

Unit 1

Countable Nouns :
Plural Forms of Regular Nouns (1)

可數名詞：規則名詞的複數形（1）

1 表示人、事、物、地方名稱的詞彙就是**名詞**。有些名詞可用數量計算；有些名詞不可以。可用數量計算的名詞稱為**可數名詞**，不能計算的稱為**不可數名詞**。

可數

a dog 狗　　　　**an apple** 蘋果

不可數

hair 頭髮　　　　**snow** 雪

2 **可數名詞**通常有**單數**（singular）和**複數**（plural）兩種形式。

單數（一個）　　　　複數（兩個以上）

a cat 一隻貓　　　　**four cats** 四隻貓

one hairbrush　　　two hairbrushes
一支梳子　　　　　兩支梳子
one television　　　two televisions
一台電視　　　　　兩台電視
a scanner　　　　　two scanners
一台掃描器　　　　兩台掃描器

3 大部分**名詞**的**複數形**是在字尾加 **s**。

student 學生　　　　students

- book 書　　→ 1 _____
- phone 電話　→ 2 _____
- table 桌子　→ 3 _____

4 當名詞字尾是 **s**、**x**、**z**、**sh** 或 **ch** 時，複數形加 **es**。

glass 玻璃杯　　　　glasses

fox → foxes 狐狸
quiz → quizzes 測驗
lunch → lunches 午餐
bush → bushes 灌木

字尾 s 和 es 的發音

❶ 名詞字尾發**無聲子音**（/f/、/k/、/p/、/t/）時，s 的讀音為 /s/。
- cups /kʌps/ 杯子　• banks /bæŋks/ 銀行

❷ 名詞字尾發**有聲子音**或**母音**時，s 的讀音為 /z/。
- computers /kəmˋpjutɚz/ 電腦
- dogs /dɔgz/ 狗

❸ 名詞字尾是 s、x、z、ch、sh 時，es 的讀音為 /ɪz/。
- bosses /ˋbɔsɪz/ 老闆
- sandwiches /ˋsændwɪtʃɪz/ 三明治

1

請將右列單數名詞改成「複數」形態。

1. dog ....
2. star ....
3. dot ....
4. glass ....
5. clock ....
6. witch ....
7. fax ....
8. banana ....
9. fuzz ....
10. crown ....
11. mop ....
12. dish ....
13. mug ....
14. sponge ....
15. slash ....
16. kite ....
17. ruler ....
18. branch ....
19. box ....
20. fan ....

2

選出圖中各種物品或身體部位所對應的名詞，並寫出它們的複數形。

shoe
hand
tree
path
shirt
plant
leg

1. ....
2. ....
3. ....
4. ....
5. ....
6. ....
7. ....

3

將右列名詞改為複數形，並依字尾 s 或 es 的發音填入正確的空格內。

watch
mother
cat
lunch
month
eraser
job
fox
park
store
bush
cup

1 /s/
....
....
....
....
....

2 /z/
....
....
....
....
....

3 /ɪz/
watches
....
....
....

Part 1 Nouns and Articles 名詞和冠詞

Unit 2

Countable Nouns :
Plural Forms of Regular Nouns (2)

可數名詞：規則名詞的複數形（2）

1 名詞字尾是「**子音＋y**」時，複數形須去 y 加 ies。

baby 嬰兒

babies

lady → ladies 女士
cherry → cherries 櫻桃
country → countries 國家
story → stories 故事

- candy 糖果 →¹ ....
- city 城市 →² ....

2 字尾是 **f** 或 **fe** 的名詞，複數形須去掉 f 或 fe，再加上 ves。也有例外。

leaf → leaves 葉子
knife → knives 刀子
thief → thieves 小偷

例外　直接加 s

▲ a giraffe
◀ two giraffes

giraffe 有兩種複數形式：
① 字尾加 s（giraffes）
② 單複數同形（two giraffe）

- half 一半 →³ ....
- wife 妻子 →⁴ ....

10

3 某些字尾是「**子音＋o**」的名詞，複數形要加上 es，但並非全部如此。

tomato → tomatoes 番茄
potato → potatoes 馬鈴薯
echo → echoes 回音
hero → heroes 英雄

例外
- photo → photos 照片
- piano → pianos 鋼琴

4 字尾如果是「**母音＋o**」的名詞，複數形只要加 s。

kangaroo 有兩種複數形式：
① 字尾加 s（two kangaroos）
② 單複數同形（two kangaroo）

kangaroos

kangaroo 袋鼠

zoo → zoos 動物園
radio → radios 收音機
video → videos 影片

5 某些名詞永遠都是以**複數**形出現。

scissors 剪刀

clothes 衣服

jeans 牛仔褲

glasses 眼鏡

shorts 短褲

- thanks 感謝
- billiards 撞球
- news 新聞
- earnings 收入
- underpants 女用內褲
- briefs 短內褲
- pants 褲子〔美〕
- trousers 長褲〔英〕
- physics 物理學
- mathematics 數學

Practice

1

請將右列單數名詞改成「複數」形態。

1. party _____
2. leaf _____
3. photo _____
4. county _____
5. army _____

6. spy _____
7. wolf _____
8. tuxedo _____
9. shelf _____
10. piano _____

2

找出必須以複數形表現的物品，並寫出正確的名稱。其他的請打╳。

1. _____

2. _____

3. _____

4. _____

5. _____

3

將錯誤的句子打╳，並寫出正確的句子。若句子無誤，則在方框內打✓。

1. I took some photos of the lake yesterday.

☐ _____

2. The scissors are in the drawer.

☐ _____

3. Be careful. Those knifes are very sharp.

☐ _____

4. Leafs keep falling from the trees.

☐ _____

5. People say cats have nine lifes.

☐ _____

6. I can't find the cloth I wore yesterday.

☐ _____

7. My father needs to wear glass to read newspapers.

☐ _____

8. You can find three librarys in this city.

☐ _____

Unit 3

Countable Nouns:
Irregular Nouns and Other Plural Nouns

可數名詞：不規則名詞與其他複數名詞

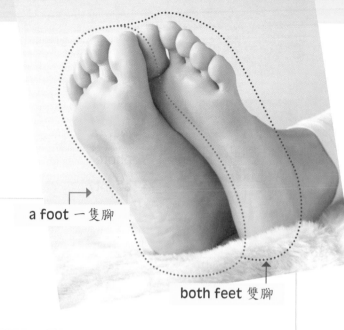

a foot 一隻腳

both feet 雙腳

1 某些名詞的複數形為**不規則變化**。

a child 小孩　　seven children

a mouse 老鼠　　three mice

單數		複數	
man	→	men	男人
woman	→	women	女人
goose	→	geese	鵝
louse	→	lice	虱子
tooth	→	teeth	牙齒
ox	→	oxen	牛

2 某些名詞的**單複數同形**，它們也屬於不規則變化的名詞。

one sheep 一隻羊　　many sheep 許多隻羊

單數	複數
one deer 一頭鹿	→ two deer
one species 一個物種	→ two ¹ _____
one aircraft 一架飛機	→ two ² _____
one bison 一頭野牛	→ two ³ _____
one moose 一頭麋鹿	→ two ⁴ _____

3 魚類的複數形有兩種：fish 和 fishes。指**同類魚**或**泛指魚**時，複數形只能用 **fish**；指**多種不同類的魚**時，通常也用 **fish**，但也可以用 **fishes**。

one fish 一條魚　　three fish
　　　　　　　　　三條魚

three fish / three fishes 三種魚

單數	複數
one salmon 一條鮭魚	→ three salmon/salmons 三條鮭魚
one trout 一條鱒魚	→ two ⁵ _____ 兩條鱒魚

Practice

1

寫出右列各種名詞的複數形。

1. .... 2. .... 3. ....

4. .... 5. .... 6. ....

2

選出正確答案。

.... 1. Bob used to count _____ to get to sleep.
　　Ⓐ a sheep 　　Ⓑ sheeps 　　Ⓒ sheep

.... 2. Who are those _____ standing in front of the gate?
　　Ⓐ woman 　　Ⓑ women 　　Ⓒ womans

.... 3. Mom told me to brush my _____ twice a day.
　　Ⓐ tooth 　　Ⓑ tooths 　　Ⓒ teeth

.... 4. Rhinos and pandas are two of the endangered _____.
　　Ⓐ species 　　Ⓑ specieses 　　Ⓒ specy

.... 5. Sometimes _____ are not afraid of cats.
　　Ⓐ mouse 　　Ⓑ mouses 　　Ⓒ mice

.... 6. Some _____ in that remote village do not have enough food to eat.
　　Ⓐ children 　　Ⓑ child 　　Ⓒ childs

.... 7. Jim likes to jog in bare _____.
　　Ⓐ foot 　　Ⓑ feet 　　Ⓒ foots

.... 8. The airline bought six _____ from France.
　　Ⓐ aircraft 　　Ⓑ aircrafts 　　Ⓒ aircreft

Unit 4

A, an
不定冠詞

1 冠詞是一種用來修飾名詞的詞，分為「定冠詞」the 和「不定冠詞」a、an，它們的功能很像形容詞。在非特定的**單數可數名詞**前面通常要加**不定冠詞 a 或 an**。

a tree 一棵樹　　an elephant 一頭大象

Have you ever eaten a worm?
你吃過蟲嗎？

2 a 和 an 只用於「單數可數名詞」前面。複數名詞前面不可以加 a 或 an。

We saw two turtles.
我們看到兩隻海龜。

Detective Conan and Demon Slayer are Japanese cartoons.
《名偵探柯南》和《鬼滅之刃》都是日本卡通。

3 a 和 an 可以用來分類人物、地方或事物。

A blog is an online web log.
部落格是一種網路日誌。

A whale is a mammal.
鯨魚是哺乳類動物。

4 字首發音為「**子音**」時（如 b、c、d、f 和 g 等），前面的不定冠詞用 a；字首發音為「**母音**」時（如 a、e、i、o 和 u 等），前面的不定冠詞則用 **an**。

a	an
 a box 一個盒子	an ax 一把斧頭
a cop 一名警察	 an ear 一隻耳朵
a dandelion 一株蒲公英	an icon 一個圖像
a flop 一聲噗通	 an otter 一隻水獺
a grab 一把抓	an uncle 一位叔叔

5 有些字的**字首拼寫雖然是子音，卻發母音**；有些字的字首**拼寫雖然是母音，卻發子音**。要用 a 或 an，請以發音為準。

an honest alien　　　a UFO 一個飛碟
一位誠懇的外星人

↳ 字首的 h 有時不發音，這個字就變成母音開頭，所以前面要用 an。

↳ u 的發音有時為 /ju/，是子音，所以前面要用 a。

字首 h
an hour 一小時
a herd 一群

字首 u
an umbrella 一把雨傘
a universe 一個宇宙

Practice

1

用 a 或 an 寫出 **Lydia** 和 **Trent** 在超市裡購買的商品名稱。

lightbulb

orange

magazine

umbrella

lamp

fish

ice cube tray

Lydia bought . . .

Trent bought . . .

2

自列表選出適當的詞彙，加上 **a** 或 **an**，完成右列句子。

art museum

glass of beer

owl

cup of coffee

café

cab

opera

1. I could walk home, but I would rather take _____.

2. We don't have any wine. Do you want _____?

3. I'm having an espresso. Would you like _____?

4. Have you ever been to _____?

5. She spent more than 5 years composing _____ based on a novel about Africa.

6. We had a lunch at _____ in Montmartre.

7. In her dream she saw _____ sitting on a branch of a tree.

Unit 5

A, an, the
不定冠詞和定冠詞

1 a、an 稱為**不定冠詞**，用於**非特指的名詞前**。當我們用 a、an 時，並沒有要對方清楚知道所指的是哪一個。

There's a movie theater near here.
這附近有間電影院。

Let's watch a horror movie.
我們去看恐怖片吧。

- Are you going to watch ¹_____ action movie?
  你要去看動作片嗎？
- Let's dine in ²_____ Chinese restaurant tonight.
  我們今天晚上去吃中國菜吧。

2 the 稱為**定冠詞**，用來**特別指某一個名詞**。用 the 表示你認為對方清楚知道所指的是哪一個。

That's Mark standing outside the theater.
馬克正站在那間戲院的外面。

The laptop I just bought was expensive.
我剛買的筆記型電腦很貴。

- We rented two movies. Let's watch ³_____ Chris movie first.
  我們租了兩部片子，先來看克里斯演的那部吧。
- Let's go to ⁴_____ newly-opened Italian restaurant.
  我們去那家新開的義大利餐廳吧。

3 再來比較一次用 a/an 和 the 的差別。

Are you going to watch a movie?
你打算看部電影嗎？ ↳ 並不確定是哪一部電影。

Are you going to watch the movie? 你要看這部電影嗎？
↳ 確定知道是哪一部電影。

There's a talk show at eight tonight.
今天晚上八點有個脫口秀。

Sam is watching *The Ellen Show*.
山姆正在看艾倫秀。

4 此外，我們經常在文章中第一次提到某物時用 a/an，再次提及時用 the。

When Jane entered the forest, she saw a unicorn. She followed the unicorn to a green lake.
珍走進森林，看到一隻獨角獸，於是她尾隨獨角獸，來到一座綠色的湖泊邊。

Ted： Kevin's father bought a bicycle for him last week.

Susan： Really? Is the bicycle expensive?

泰德： 凱文的爸爸上星期買了一台腳踏車給他。

蘇珊： 真的嗎？那台腳踏車貴不貴啊？

Practice

1

用 a、an 或 the
填空，完成對話。

1. David: Is there _____ public library in town?
   Janet: Yes, there is one.
   David: Would you like to go to _____ library tomorrow?
   Janet: OK.

2. Joe: Where is _____ remote control?
   Kay: _____ remote control is on _____ table.
   Joe: Where is _____ gamepad?
   Kay: _____ gamepad is on _____ sofa.

3. Nancy: Did you see that woman?
   Phil: What woman?
   Nancy: _____ woman who is looking at _____ cellphone.
   Phil: Oh, yes.

4. Amy: Where is Mom?
   Tony: She's in _____ kitchen.
   Amy: What is she doing in _____ kitchen?
   Tony: She's making _____ sandwich.

5. Jim: How do you like your new office building?
   Kelly: I like it. It has _____ big conference room.
   Jim: Do you use _____ conference room a lot?
   Kelly: Yes, I use it every day.

2

請選出正確的答案
填入空格。

1. **a channel**　**the channel**
   Ⓐ Please change _____.
   Ⓑ Please find _____ with something good on it.

2. **a movie**　**the movie**
   Ⓐ Do you want to watch _____ on cable?
   Ⓑ Do you want to watch _____ we talked about last night?

3. **a sandwich**　**the sandwich**
   Ⓐ Do you want to eat _____?
   Ⓑ Are you going to eat _____ I made for you?

4. **a soda**　**the soda**
   Ⓐ Do you want _____ with your sandwich?
   Ⓑ Do you want _____ you bought at the store?

Unit 6

Uncountable Nouns
不可數名詞

---

1 不可用**數量計算**的名詞，則稱為不可數名詞，前面不可以加數字。

~~one~~ powder
~~two~~ powder 粉末

~~one~~ makeup
~~two~~ makeup 化妝品

---

2 不可數名詞意指無法分成個體的名詞，表示**概念、狀態、品質、感情或物質材料**。

cheese 起司   coffee 咖啡

- beer 啤酒
- butter 奶油
- beauty 美麗
- courage 勇氣
- love 愛

- horror 恐懼
- luggage 行李
- equipment 裝備
- cosmetics 化妝品
- truth 真理

---

3 不可數名詞只有一種形式，通常作**單數形**，沒有複數形。

homework 功課
~~homeworks~~

milk 牛奶
~~milks~~

---

4 不可數名詞前面可不加任何限定詞，動詞必須使用**單數動詞**，如 be 動詞 is。可數名詞則視名詞的單複數決定動詞的單複數，複數使用 are。

Is education free in your country?
在你們國家受教育是免費的嗎？

Money is important for basic commodities.
↳ 不可數名詞 education 和 money 前面不加限定詞，並使用單數動詞 is。

要買到基本的生活用品，錢是很重要的。

比較

Where is your grammar book?
你的文法書在哪裡？
Where are your grammar books?
↳ 可數名詞視單複數決定用 is 或 are。
你的文法書在哪裡？

錯誤

✘ His furnitures are old. 他的家具都很舊。
✘ His meat are fresh. 他賣的肉都很新鮮。

---

5 有些名詞會同時具有可數和不可數的形式，但意義不同。

How many cakes do you want to get?
         ↳ 指一塊一塊的蛋糕
你想要幾個蛋糕？

Cake is fattening. 蛋糕使人發胖。
   ↳ 指蛋糕整體

Who is that lady with long hair?
那個長頭髮的小姐是誰？   ↳ 指頭髮整體

There is a hair in my soup.
      ↳ 指一根一根的頭髮
我的湯裡有一根頭髮。

There are some dog hairs on the sofa.
沙發上有一些狗毛。   ↳ 指一根一根的毛髮

Practice

1

將右列單字歸類為可數或不可數名詞，並在可數名詞前正確的加上 a 或 an，不可數名詞則不用加。

可數

不可數

comb

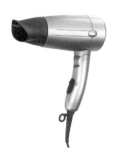
newspaper

hairdryer   shampoo

sugar

bread

2

在第一格填上正確的動詞（is 或 are），並在第二格填上正確的冠詞（a 或 an），若不需要冠詞請打 ✗。

1. There _____ _____ some water in the bottle.

2. There _____ _____ some cream rinse in the bathroom.

3. There _____ _____ jar of cold cream on the sink.

4. Those women _____ _____ buyers for the company.

5. That man _____ _____ sales representative.

6. That _____ _____ beautiful bottle.

7. That _____ _____ inexpensive makeup case.

8. There _____ _____ sale on eyeliners.

3

改正右列句子的錯誤，若句子無誤，則在後面寫上 OK。

1. How often do you cut your hairs? _____ *hair* _____

2. I am thinking of buying some jewelries. _____

3. Where do you buy your makeups? _____

4. How much skin cream do you use? _____

5. I am buying some cosmetic at a department store.

   _____

6. It takes a lot of courages for Tom to do this. _____

7. Beauty is only skin deep. _____

Unit 7

Counting an Uncountable Noun
不可數名詞的計算

1 不可數名詞的**數量**，可以用可計算的**量詞**來表示。

量詞

- **bottle** 瓶
- **tube** 管
- **box** 箱；盒
- **can** 罐
- **jar** 廣口瓶
- **packet** 包；袋
- **bowl** 碗
- **bar** 塊
- **carton** 紙盒
- **stick** 根
- **pot** 壺
- **piece** 個；件

two tubes of
toothpaste
兩條牙膏

a bottle of
perfume
一瓶香水

a box of
chocolate
一盒巧克力

a bar of
soap
一塊肥皂

a can of
hairspray
一罐髮霧

a bowl of
rice
一碗飯

a jar of
jam
一罐果醬

a carton of
milk
一瓶牛奶

three sticks of
incense
三支香

2 在不可數名詞前，常用 some 作限定詞，但**不能用 a 或 an**。

We have <u>some</u> **information** about him.
我們有一些關於他的消息。

There's <u>some</u> **rice** on the counter.
櫃臺上有一些米。

錯誤

- We have ~~an information~~.
- There's ~~a rice~~ on the counter.

- We need [1]_____ advice.
  我們需要一點建議。
- Please buy me [2]_____ bread.
  請幫我買一點麵包。

3 不可數名詞前面用 some 表示**數量不確定**，用量詞表示**具體的數量**。

數量不確定	具體的數量
She's got some wine. 她有一些葡萄酒。	She's got a bottle of wine. 她有一瓶葡萄酒。
There's some spaghetti on the stove. 爐子上有一些義大利麵。	There are two boxes of spaghetti in the cupboard. 櫃子裡有兩盒義大利麵。

比較

a stick of
glue

a bottle of
glue

a tube of
glue

Practice

1

請將物品正確的數量搭配表中量詞填入空格；不需要使用 of 片語的，請填入 some。注意量詞的單複數。

bowl of
stick of
jar of
tube of
bar of
carton of
can of
bottle of
some
piece of

1 *two bottles of*
wine

2 _____
chocolate

3 _____
jam

4 _____
paint

5 _____
spaghetti

6 _____
soup

7 _____
juice

8 _____
butter

9 _____
paper

10 _____
Coke

2

改正右列句子的錯誤。

1. Where can I buy a chocolate?

_____

2. How many luggages do you have?

_____

3. It's too quiet. I need a music.

_____

4. How many bowls of perfume did you get?

_____

5. Can you buy me two breads?

_____

6. My brother wants to buy a new furniture.

_____

Unit 8

Talking in General
名詞的泛指用法

1 一般來說，名詞前若沒有 the，是泛指事物的**總體**。

Pubs **are noisy.**
酒吧很嘈雜。

Apples **are good for health.**
蘋果對健康很好。

Do you like going to cafés?
你喜歡去咖啡廳嗎？

- 1 ＿＿＿＿＿ **are expensive.** 車子很貴。
- 2 ＿＿＿＿＿ **are grass-eating animals.**
  山羊是草食性動物。

2 名詞前面加 the，是特別指某**具體事物**。

Please try the cookies.
請吃吃看這些餅乾。

Take the apples.
拿這些蘋果吧。

- 3 ＿＿＿＿＿ **in this showroom are**
  very expensive.
  這個展場裡的車子很貴。

3 再來比較一次有沒有 the 的差別。

I love to eat sushi.
我喜歡吃壽司。

The **sushi is not fresh.**
這些壽司不新鮮。

Furniture **is hard to move.**
家具很難搬移。

The **furniture is in the truck.**
這批家具在貨車上。

- 4 ＿＿＿＿＿ are
  here to see you.
  警察來探視你了。

Practice

1

貓貓都喜歡些什麼？
根據圖示，並利用下
表提示，造句解釋貓
貓喜歡什麼和不喜歡
什麼。

balls of yarn
showers
dogs
fish
boxes
vets

1. _____

2. _____

3. _____

4. _____

5. _____

6. _____

2

選出正確的答案填入
空格中。

1. Coffee   The coffee

   Ⓐ _____ keeps you awake at night.

   Ⓑ _____ is in the pot next to the cups.

2. money   the money

   Ⓐ You need _____ to live.

   Ⓑ I gave _____ to the landlord.

3. Rice   The rice

   Ⓐ _____ is the most important grain crop.

   Ⓑ _____ is cooked with butter and parsley.

4. attendance   the class attendance

   Ⓐ The class has low _____.

   Ⓑ I entered _____ into the computer.

Unit 9

Proper Nouns
專有名詞

> 名稱中有「. . . of . . .」者，則一定要加 the。
>
> I studied at the University of Michigan.
> 我在密西根大學念書。
>
> I went on vacation to the Bay of Fundy.
> 我到芬地灣度假。

1 特定人、事物、地方、國家的名稱屬
於專有名詞，首字母必須**大寫**。

| *The New York Times* 紐約時報 | Shawn Mendes 尚恩‧曼德斯 | Australia 澳洲 | Tower Bridge 倫敦塔橋 |

2 大多數專有名詞的前面**不加** the。

❶ **Names** 人名
~~The~~ Mike is my uncle. 麥克是我叔叔。

❷ **Days of the week** 星期
Tomorrow is ~~the~~ Saturday. 明天是星期六。

❸ **Months of the year** 月分
My favorite month is ~~the~~ September.
九月是我最喜歡的月分。

❹ **Languages and nationalities**
語言和國籍
~~The~~ Russian is a difficult language.
俄語是一種很困難的語言。

❺ **Countries, continents, and regions**
國家、洲和地區名稱
Did you like your trip to ~~the~~ France?
你喜歡那趟法國之行嗎？
~~The~~ Canada is in ~~the~~ North America.
加拿大在北美洲。

❻ **Villages, towns, and cities**
村、鎮和城市名稱
~~The~~ Toronto is the biggest city in Canada.
多倫多是加拿大最大的城市。

❼ **Street / road / avenue names**
街、道路、大道名
I have a friend who lives on ~~the~~ Washington
Street. 我有個朋友住在華盛頓街。

❽ **Place names** 地方名
I know a student at ~~the~~ Seattle University.
我認識一名西雅圖大學的學生。

❾ **Lake** 湖泊
~~The~~ Lake Michigan is located entirely
within the United States.
密西根湖完全位於美國境內。

3 有些專有名詞必須**加** the。

❶ **Hotels, restaurants, and pubs** 飯店、
餐廳和酒吧
The Ritz Carlton is a famous hotel.
麗池卡爾登度假酒店是間知名的飯店。

❷ **Cinemas** 電影院
Tenet is showing at the New Art Cinema.
《天能》正在新藝術電影院上映。

❸ **Theaters** 劇院
How do I get to the Goodman Theater?
我要如何到古德曼劇院？

❹ **Seas and oceans** 海和洋
Is the Mediterranean a sea or an ocean?
地中海是海還是洋？

❺ **Rivers** 河流
The longest river in South America is
the Amazon. 亞馬遜河是南美洲最長的河。

Practice

1

請在必要的地方，填
上 the；若不必要，
則畫上「╳」。

1. _____ University of Cambridge
2. _____ Jason
3. _____ Wednesday
4. _____ February
5. _____ Sheraton Hotel
6. _____ France
7. _____ Asia
8. _____ Whitewater Pub
9. _____ Tokyo
10. _____ Budapest Café
11. _____ River Thames

12. _____ Oprah Winfrey
13. _____ West River
14. _____ Pacific Ocean
15. _____ Los Angeles County Museum of Art
16. _____ Lake Michigan
17. _____ Century Cinema
18. _____ Jackson Avenue
19. _____ Ireland
20. _____ Korean

2

將右列句子改寫為
正確的句子。

1. "What are you reading?" "I'm reading *china post*."

→ _____

_____

2. Is mary going to japan with you?

→ _____

3. jane has a project due in the october.

→ _____

4. Why don't we see the latest movie in miramar cinema?

→ _____

_____

5. Is the yellow river the longest river in china?

→ _____

6. Excuse me, how do I get to the maple street?

→ _____

7. Are you going to evanston public library?

→ _____

Part 1 Nouns and Articles 名詞和冠詞

Unit 10

Expressions With and Without "the" (1)
加 the 與不加 the 的情況（1）

1 娛樂消遣的場所和活動名稱要加 the。

go to the movie theater 去電影院

be at the movie theater 在電影院

listen to the radio 聽廣播

be on the radio 廣播中

watch the broadcast 看轉播

will be in the broadcast 即將轉播

We go to the theater whenever there is a good movie.
只要有好電影，我們就會去電影院看。

How often do you go to the cinema for art films? 你多久會去戲院看一次藝術電影？

2 電視前面不加 the。但是若 TV 指一台具體的「電視機」時，則需加 the。

They're watching TV. 他們在看電視。

The movie is on TV tonight.
這部電影今晚會在電視上播映。

Your glasses are next to the TV.
你的眼鏡在電視機旁邊。

3 天氣類型需加 the。

I hate getting caught in the rain.
我討厭淋雨。

I wear sunscreen if I am going to be in the sun.
如果會曬到太陽，我就會擦隔離霜。

The weather is nasty today.
今天天氣很差。

4 三餐前面不加 the。

have/eat breakfast 吃早餐

have/eat lunch 吃午餐

have/eat dinner 吃晚餐

It is important to eat ~~the~~ breakfast every morning.
每天早上吃早餐是很重要的。

5 帶有介系詞 on 或 by 的交通工具前面不加 the。

on foot 走路

by car 開車

by bicycle 騎腳踏車

by train 搭火車

by scooter 騎機車

by subway 搭地鐵

by bus 搭公車

by plane 搭飛機

Going on ~~the~~ foot is much better than taking a bus. 走路比搭公車好多了。

If you go by ~~the~~ car, be prepared for traffic jams.
假如你開車去，要有塞車的心理準備。

Practice

1

依據圖示，自下表選出適當的詞彙，完成右列句子，並視需要加上 the。

breakfast
TV
radio
rain
theater
car

1. What's that music you're listening to on ....?

2. Last weekend, Tom and Patti went to ....

3. It'll be quicker if we go by ....

4. Every morning we have cereal and milk for ....

5. The laundry got all wet because of ....

6. Is there anything good on .... tonight?

2

在必要的地方加 the；在不必要的地方畫上「✗」。

1. This morning I got caught by .... rain.
2. When was the last time you went to .... cinema?
3. I'm so busy that I don't have time to eat .... lunch.
4. While I was driving, I heard a beautiful song on .... radio.
5. We could go on .... foot, but going by .... cab will be faster.
6. There is a fashion show on .... TV tonight.

Unit **11**

Expressions With and Without "the" (2)
加 the 與不加 the 的情況（2）

1 樂器名稱需加 the。

play the **cello** 彈大提琴

play the **piano** 彈鋼琴

play the **guitar** 彈吉他

He has been playing the **violin** for 12 years.
他拉小提琴已經 12 年了。

2 以下泛稱性的自然環境地點，
一般要加 the。

I like living in the country.
我喜歡住在鄉下。

He commutes from the suburbs to the city every day. 他每天從郊區通勤到城裡。

They have a house in the city.
他們在市區有間房子。

I used to swim in the sea.
我以前常在海裡游泳。

3 某些社會機構名稱不用加 the。

go to **church**
上教堂作禮拜
at **church**
上教堂作禮拜
in **church**
上教堂作禮拜

go to **school** 上學
be at **school** 在上學
（相對於在家或在校外）
be in **school** 在上學
（相對於有工作）

go to **court** 上法庭
be at **court** 在庭上
be in **court** 在庭上

go to **jail** 去坐牢
be in **jail** 進牢裡
go to **prison** 進監獄
be in **prison** 進監獄

- Right now he is [1] _____.
  此刻他在教堂作禮拜。
- When do you have to be
  [2] _____?
  你什麼時候要到學校上課？

4 有些社會機構名稱可加 the，也可不加。

go to (a) **hospital**
go to the **hospital**
去醫院
↳ 美式須用 the：
  go to the hospital

go to (a) **university**
go to the **university**
上大學（和 school、church 的用法一樣）
↳ go to the university
  指特定某所大學
  go to university
  泛指「上大學」

Practice

1

依據圖示，自下表選出適當的詞彙，完成右列句子，並視需要加上 the。

church
university
violin
court
hospital
city

1. Do you prefer to live in the country or in ....

2. She wants to learn to play ....

3. I didn't see you in .... last Sunday.

4. Jimmy left his home and went to .... last month.

5. The lawyer spent a lot of time at .... for this case.

6. Grandma is sick and has been in .... for a week.

2

在必要的地方加 the；在不必要的地方畫上「✕」。

1. I love the beach, but I don't like lying in .... sun.
2. They go to .... church once a year on Christmas Eve.
3. He can play .... guitar, ... bass, and .... piano.
4. He is studying electronics in .... college.
5. First he was in .... jail and now he is in .... prison.
6. Are you going to show your guest around .... town?
7. Terri and Craig love riding bicycles in .... countryside.
8. They are going to .... court for a murder case.

Unit **12**

Other Expressions Without "the"
其他不需要加 the 的情況

1 從事某種**球類運動**不用加 the。

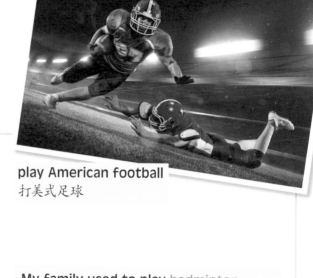

play American football
打美式足球

play basketball 打籃球

play volleyball 打排球

play soccer 踢足球

play baseball 打棒球

My family used to play badminton every Sunday.
我家人以前每週日都會去打羽球。

I'm learning tennis. 我在學網球。

Is golf very popular in your country?
你們國家盛行高爾夫球嗎？

2 某些**慣用語**前面不加 the。

go to work 上班   be at work 工作中
go home 回家   be at home 在家
go to bed 去睡覺   be in bed 在床上

I have to go to work early this morning.
我今天一早就得去上班。

3 **學科**的名稱前面不加 the。

My favorite subject is the math.
數學是我最喜歡的科目。

Daniel is studying the geography.
丹尼爾正在唸地理。

I'm good at physics and chemistry.
我擅長的科目是物理和化學。

4 **季節**名稱通常不加 the，但也有例外。

It will soon be spring again.
春天又將到臨。

My family likes to relax on a tropical island in summer.
我們家夏天時喜歡到熱帶島嶼上度假。

I love autumn the best.
秋天是我最愛的季節。

例外

She will be leaving for New York in the fall.
她將於這個秋天啟程前往紐約。
↳ fall 無論如何都要加 the。

Joan and Matt first met in the winter of 2005.
瓊和麥特初次相遇於 2005 年的冬天。
↳ 特別指某個冬天（春天、夏天、秋天）時就要加 the。

Practice

1

依據圖示，自下表選出適當的詞彙，完成右列句子，並視需要加上 the。

math
tennis
home
work
winter

1. She's not home right now. She's at _____ .

2. Hey, why not play _____ with me this afternoon?

3. Birds will fly south before _____ comes.

4. Dora's always been good at _____ .

5. She decided to cancel her date and just stay at _____ and read.

2

在必要的地方加 the；在不必要的地方畫上「╳」。

1. If I'm tired, I go to _____ bed and sleep 12 hours straight.
2. She will be going to _____ college in _____ fall.
3. I love _____ autumn better than _____ summer.
4. Billy had surgery this morning, and he has to stay in _____ bed for the next two days.
5. Is _____ soccer popular among the students in your class?
6. Are you good at _____ English grammar?

3

依據事實，回答右列問題。

1. What's your favorite sport?
   → _____
2. What's your favorite subject?
   → _____
3. What's your favorite season?
   → _____
4. What subject do you dislike the most?
   → _____
5. What season do you dislike the most?
   → _____

Unit 13

Possessive : 's

所有格 : 's

1 用來表示所有權或彼此關係的詞彙或格式，稱為**所有格**。

Susan's **apples**
蘇珊的蘋果

John's **lunch**
約翰的午餐

2 **單數名詞和人名**的後面加「 's 」，即成為所有格。

Cathy's **cat** 凱西的貓

his sister's **book** 他姐的書

3 **複數名詞**或**複數人名**的所有格只要加「 ' 」。

the brothers' **restaurant**
哥哥們的餐廳

the Jones' **dinner party**
瓊斯家的晚宴

4 **字尾不是 s 結尾**的不規則複數名詞，也是加「 's 」變成所有格。

the women's **snack**
這些女人們的點心

the children's **meal**
孩子們的餐點

比較

my friend's **party**
我朋友的派對 一個朋友

my friends' **party**
我朋友們的派對 多個朋友

5 在**人和人**或**人和物**之間加所有格，表示**人和人**或**人和物**之間的關係。

Lily's **father** 莉莉的父親

my brother's **shirt** 我哥的襯衫

- That's ¹ _____ car.
  那是我朋友的車。
- That's ² _____ sister.
  那是喬的姊妹。

6 如果**前後文的主詞**都很清楚，則所有格「 's 」或「 ' 」後面的名詞可以省略。

Whose coffee is this? It's Jim's.
這是誰的咖啡？吉姆的。 ↳ = Jim's coffee

Whose cake is this? It's Jan's.
這是誰的蛋糕？是珍的。 ↳ = Jan's cake

所有格「 's 」字尾發音

❶ 名詞字尾發**無聲子音**（ /f/、/k/、/p/、/t/ ）時，「 's 」或「 s' 」的讀音為 /s/。
- a giraffe's **long neck** 長頸鹿的長脖子
  /dʒəˈræfs/

❷ 名詞字尾發**有聲子音**或**母音**時，「 's 」讀音為 /z/。
- my brother's **backpack** 我哥哥的背包
  /ˈbrʌðəz/

❸ 名詞字尾是 s、x、z、ch、sh 時，「 's 」或「 s' 」的讀音為 /ɪz/。
- my boss's **desk** 我老闆的桌子
  /ˈbɔsɪz/
- the fox's **tail** 狐狸的尾巴
  /ˈfaksɪz/
- Josh's **reward points** 喬許的兌換點數
  /ˈdʒaʃɪz/

1

右列物品可能會是誰的？請依圖示，分別用完整句子和簡答來回答問題。

 Catherine

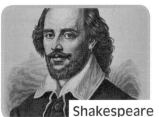 Shakespeare

 Kevin Durant

 Tim Cook

 the wizard

 Kiki

1

Whose key is it?

It is _Catherine's key_ .

It is _Catherine's_ .

2

Whose collar is it?

It is _____.

It is _____.

3

Whose pen and ink is it?

It is _____
_____.

It is _____.

4

Whose briefcase is it?

It is _____.

It is _____.

5

Whose magic wand is it?

It is _____
_____.

It is _____.

6

Whose basketball is it?

It is _____
_____.

It is _____.

2

將表中的名詞改為所有格，並依字尾「's」的發音填入正確的空格內。

Jennifer
student
Alice
dish
bottle
aunt
Jeff
ox
lion
tank
kid
tax

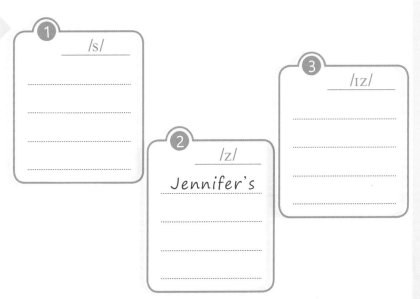

1 /s/
_____
_____
_____
_____
_____

2 /z/
Jennifer's
_____
_____
_____

3 /ɪz/
_____
_____
_____
_____

Unit **14**

Possessive: the . . . of . . .
所有格：the . . . of . . .

1 通常**無生物**的所有格要用「of . . .」來表示。

the window of the room 房間的窗戶

the end of the road 路的盡頭

the cover of the magazine 雜誌的封面

- I like the color [1]_____.
  我喜歡這面牆壁的顏色。
- Janet is a student [2]_____.
  珍奈特是這所學校的學生。

2 表示**時間**或**度量**的名詞，則必須用「's」或「'」來表示所有格。

today's schedule 今天的行程

four hours' work 四小時的工作

a year's membership 一年的會員資格

two dollars' worth 兩塊美金的價值

3 擬人化的名詞也必須用「's」或「'」來表示所有格。

heaven's will 天意

Mars' surface 火星地表

life's miracle 生命奇蹟

the world's economy 全球經濟

4 即使名詞屬於**生物**，有時也可以用「of . . .」來表示關係或所有權；但「's」或「'」的所有格形式更常見，也更為自然。

the smile of the dog = the dog's smile
狗狗的笑容　　　　　　　↳ 用法更常見、自然

the leaves of the tree
= the tree's leaves
這棵樹的葉子

the son of Tim = Tim's son
提姆的兒子

- the toys [3]_____
  = the boy's toys 男孩的玩具
- the tail [4]_____
  = the pig's tail 豬的尾巴

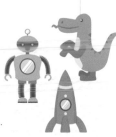

Practice

1

將右列「of . . .」的用法改寫為「's」
或「'」的所有格。

1. the schoolbag of the student

   → ....

   ....

2. the iPad of Jenny

   → ....

   ....

3. the newspaper of Grandpa

   → ....

   ....

4. the laptop of David

   → ....

   ....

5. the headphones of my sister

   → ....

   ....

6. the umbrella of my brother

   → ....

   ....

7. the cell phone of the manager

   → ....

   ....

8. the scarf of my mother

   → ....

   ....

9. the book of Liz

   → ....

   ....

2

自左右兩個列表中各選出相關的詞彙，並用「the . . . of . . .」描述它們之間的附屬關係。

pile	1. *the light of the sun*	the sun
light	2.	trash
ninth symphony	3.	the computer
keyboard	4.	the president
speech	5.	Beethoven

Unit **15** Review Test of Units 1–14
單元 1–14 總複習

1 下列物品名稱，哪些是可數名詞？哪些是不可數名詞？請在可數名詞的空格內
寫上 C（countable），不可數名詞的空格內寫上 U（uncountable）。

→ Unit 1, 6 重點複習

1	_C_ belt
2	☐ helicopter
3	☐ marker
4	☐ cloth
5	☐ mayonnaise
6	☐ cloud
7	☐ water
8	☐ castle
9	☐ bread
10	☐ dolphin
11	☐ paper
12	☐ swimming pool
13	☐ olive oil
14	☐ pearl
15	☐ sugar

2 依據題意，自圖片中選出正確的單字，改成複數名詞來填空。

→ Unit 1, 3 重點複習

1. I heard lots of .... running around above the ceiling of my room.
2. I really don't like washing ....
3. This store sells some clocks and ....
4. My little brother loves to eat .... for dessert.
5. There aren't many .... this year.
6. Do little .... drink milk from their mother?
7. .... have an important role in many fairy tales.
8. Archaeologists found several dinosaur .... on this spot.
9. Mom is cooking two .... for dinner.
10. Iris wrote several .... while she was traveling in Europe.

▲ holiday
▲ rat
▲ watch
▲ calf ▲ dish
▼ fish ▲ elf
▲ tooth
▲ jelly candy ▲ diary

3 運用圖中的單字填空，並根據內文做正確的單複數形變化，或加上 a、an、the。

→ **Unit 4–5 重點複習**

carrot

1. Give the rabbit ....
2. I left .... on the grass for the rabbit.
3. .... are a healthy food.

lion

4. They have a statue of ....
5. The statue of .... is very old.
6. .... are a symbol of power.

sugar

7. I like .... in my tea.
8. Where is ....?

banana

9. Would you like ....?
10. Who gets ....?

keyboard

11. He reached out his hands to ....
    and typed some words.
12. Can you stop at the electronics store to buy
    ....?

music

13. .... distracts me when I am
    studying.
14. What is .... you are playing?

選出符合題意的詞彙，以正確的形式（加上 a、an、the，或改為複數名詞，或完全不需要冠詞等）來填空完成句子。可重複使用詞彙。

→ Unit 1, 4–5, 8 重點複習

Johnny lives in ❶_____.
He commutes from his place to work by
❷_____ every day. He loves
playing ❸_____.
Tonight there is going to be a football game
on ❹_____. So he plans to go
❺_____ early. He will also buy two
cheeseburgers and some French fries for
❻_____. He will not go to
❼_____ until the game is over.

Muhammad is ❽_____. He
told me that ❾_____, the
longest river in the world, plays an important
role in the life of all ❿_____.
However, some geographers from
⓫_____ and Peru are claiming that
⓬_____ is the longest river
in the world by now. They are claiming that
they've found ⓭_____ of the river,
and the length of the river makes it the longest
one. Debates between ⓮_____ go
on. No matter which river is the longest one
on earth, they are popular sites for
⓯_____ from all over the world.

bed

dinner

TV

football

Egyptian

new source

Brazil

car

suburbs

Amazon River

scientist

home

tourist

Nile River

5 圈選正確的答案。
→ Unit 4–5, 8 重點複習

1. Do you have camera | a camera | an camera | some camera ?
2. We are having potatoes | a potatoes | an potatoes | some potato for dinner.
3. She has long hair | a hair | an hair | hairs .
4. Please help me carry a boxes | a box | an box | some box .
5. We already have a loaves | a loaf | an loaf | some loafs of bread.
6. There is lots of snow | a snow | an snow | snows in the mountains.
7. Where is | are your watch?
8. How many people is | are coming?
9. Is | Are this rice expensive?

6 根據題目所提供的內容，以「's」和「the . . . of . . .」這兩種形式來表達所有格；
若該題目不適合以某一形式表達，則畫上「✕」。
→ Unit 13–14 重點複習

1 Ned

suitcase

Ⓐ _Ned's suitcase_
Ⓑ _the suitcase of Ned_

2 my father

jacket

Ⓐ _____
Ⓑ _____

3 my sister

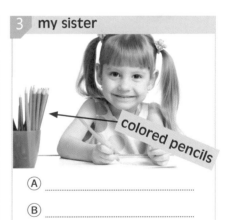

colored pencils

Ⓐ _____
Ⓑ _____

4 bathroom

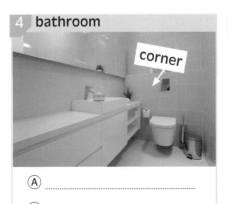

corner

Ⓐ _____
Ⓑ _____

5 Edward

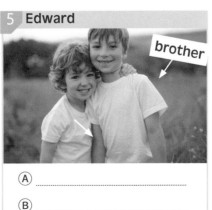

brother

Ⓐ _____
Ⓑ _____

6 vacation

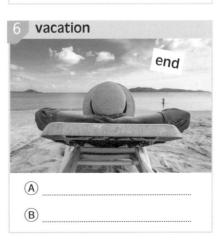

end

Ⓐ _____
Ⓑ _____

7 將下列圖中的各項物品名稱，依據其適合的量詞，填入正確的空格內。

→ Unit 7 重點複習

tuna	soy sauce	grapes	wine	luggage	shaving cream
cheese	watercolor	potato chips	jewelry	pickles	cleansing foam
tea	lotion	peanut butter	soda	coffee	salad
soup	strawberry jam	ketchup	rice	cookies	ointment

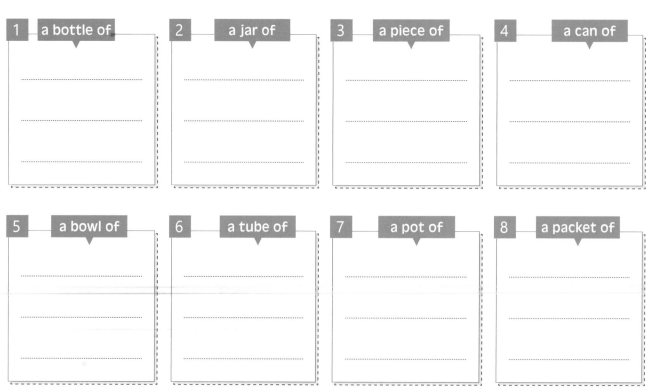

| 1 a bottle of | 2 a jar of | 3 a piece of | 4 a can of |
| 5 a bowl of | 6 a tube of | 7 a pot of | 8 a packet of |

8 下列名詞類別是否需要加「the」？在需要 the 的類別上將「the」打勾；
在不需要 the 的類別上將「the」打叉，並各舉兩個例子。

→ Unit 9-11 重點複習

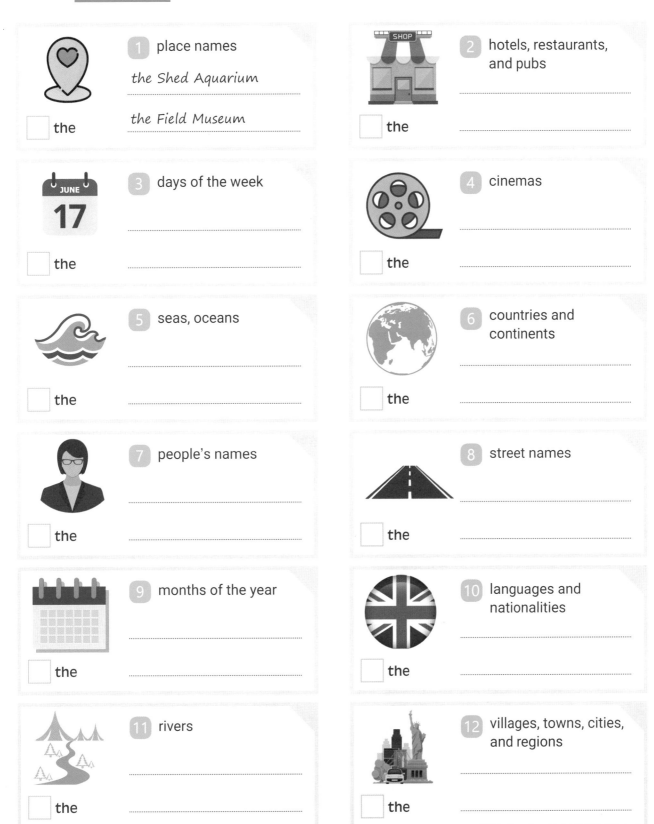

1 place names

the Shed Aquarium

the Field Museum

☐ the

2 hotels, restaurants, and pubs

☐ the

3 days of the week

☐ the

4 cinemas

☐ the

5 seas, oceans

☐ the

6 countries and continents

☐ the

7 people's names

☐ the

8 street names

☐ the

9 months of the year

☐ the

10 languages and nationalities

☐ the

11 rivers

☐ the

12 villages, towns, cities, and regions

☐ the

Unit 16

Personal Pronouns: Subject Pronouns
人稱代名詞：主詞代名詞

1 用來代替名詞的詞稱為代名詞。其中一種具有人稱區別的代名詞稱為**人稱代名詞**，用來指人或事物。

Tim is English. **He**'s from London.
                ↳ 是人稱代名詞，代替 Tim。
提姆是英國人，他是從倫敦來的。

The cell phone on the desk is **mine**.
桌上的手機是我的。   ↳ 人稱代名詞，
                                 等於 my cell
                                 phone。

2 人稱代名詞有三種型態，分別為**主詞代名詞、受詞代名詞**和**所有格代名詞**。

主詞代名詞		受詞代名詞		所有格代名詞		所有格形容詞	
I	我	me	我	mine	我的	my	我的
we	我們	us	我們	ours	我們的	our	我們的
you	你	you	你	yours	你的	your	你的
you	你們	you	你們	yours	你們的	your	你們的
he	他	him	他	his	他的	his	他的
she	她	her	她	hers	她的	her	她的
it	它	it	它			its	它的
they	他們	them	他們	theirs	他們的	their	他們的

↳ 所有格形容詞雖然不是代名詞，但是卻與所有格代名詞相關且容易混淆，請看 Unit 18 的詳細說明。

3 主詞代名詞有單數，也有複數。

4 主詞代名詞可用來表示自己、和自己對話的人、對話中已提過的人或事，以及已知事物。
在句中通常當主詞用，不能省略。

I've got a job in Los Angeles.
我在洛杉磯工作。

What are **you** looking for?
你在找什麼？

We are going to buy some fruit.
我們要去買一些水果。

Annie isn't in town. **She**'s on vacation.
安妮不在城裡，她去度假了。

Cindy and Melissa aren't on-line. **They**'re at a pub.
辛蒂和梅麗莎並沒有在線上，她們在酒吧。

5 **it** 是個**單數、中性**的主詞代名詞。可以**泛指**一般的**事物、動物**，也可以用來代表**時間、日期、天氣**和**距離**。
（確定性別的寵物，也常用 he 或 she。）

general	一般事物	**It**'s a giant ship. 那是一艘巨輪。
time	時間	**It**'s 3 o'clock. 現在時間是三點。
days	星期	**It**'s Tuesday. 今天是星期二。
weather	天氣	**It**'s rainy. 今天是雨天。
distance	距離	**It**'s 5 blocks to the bus stop. 公車站在五條街外。

◆ 主詞代名詞可以和動詞 am、is、are、have got、has got 一起縮寫。

I'm	he's	I've got	he's got
we're	she's	we've got	she's got
you're	it's	you've got	it's got
they're		they've got	

1

請依圖示，在空格處填上 I、you、he、she、it、we 或 they，完成句子。

◄ 1. _____'m on the phone.

◄ 2. _____'re taller than me.

▲ 3. _____'s got cool hair.

▲ 4. _____'s raining hard.

▲ 5. _____'s a tall building.

▲ 6. _____'re going surfing.

▲ 7. _____'re going to jump.

▲ 8. _____'s running.

▲ 9. _____'s got a new car.

2

請依圖示，在空格處填上 I、you、he、she、it、we 或 they，完成句子。

1. These are my parents. _____'re both in excellent health.

2. My dad is retired. _____'s 75 years old.

3. My mom helps take care of our kids. _____'s a big help.

4. My son is Sam. _____'s a very good student.

5. My daughter is Mary. _____'s learning to play the violin.

6. My dog is Fred. _____'s cute.

7. We just bought a summer house. _____'s in Hawaii.

8. That's us. _____'re a happy family.

Unit **17**

Personal Pronouns: Object Pronouns
人稱代名詞：受詞代名詞

1 受詞代名詞也是人稱代名詞的一種，通常作受詞用，不能省略。受詞代名詞**有單數，也有複數**。

單數		複數	
me	我	us	我們
you	你	you	你們
him	他		
her	她	them	他們
it	它		

Danny is at the party. Did you see him?
丹尼在派對裡。你有看到他嗎？

Betty and Judy are doing their homework. Can you help them?
貝蒂和茱蒂正在做功課。你可以幫她們嗎？

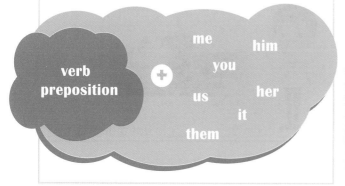

verb
preposition

+

me
you
us
him
her
it
them

2 介系詞片語中，受詞代名詞需放在**介系詞後面**。

When is Doug leaving? I want to go with him.
道格什麼時候會離開？我要跟他一起走。

Have you seen Barb? I am looking for her.
你有看到芭波嗎？我在找她。

The whole family is here. Have you talked to them? 這一家人都在這裡。你和他們談過了嗎？

3 受詞代名詞可以直接放在**動詞**（如：see、help、like）**後面**，不加介系詞。

We're waiting for Sam. Did you see him?
我們在等山姆，你看到他了嗎？   ↳ him 指的是 Sam

I'm supposed to meet my daughter here. I'm helping her **move to a new apartment.**   ↳ her 指的是 the daughter
我約好在這裡和我女兒見面，我要幫她搬家到新公寓。

Jack told me **that he was sick.**
傑克告訴我他生病了。

Jennifer doesn't like us.
珍妮佛不喜歡我們。

Did you see my headphones? I need it **right now.**
你有沒有看到我的耳機？我現在需要它。

I'll give you **a call tomorrow morning.**
我明天早上打電話給你。

I love to eat lobsters. **Do you** like them?
我喜歡吃龍蝦。你呢？   ↳ them 指的是 lobsters

• **Janet needs some help. Can you help**
  [1]_____?
  珍奈特需要幫助，你可以幫她嗎？
• **Steven and Naomi are very friendly. I like**
  [2]_____ **very much.**
  史蒂文和娜歐蜜都很和善，我很喜歡他們。

• **A Which letter is for Mary?**
  B This one is for [3]_____?
  A 哪一封是瑪莉的信？
  B 這封是她的。

• **Here are some photos of Bill and Theresa. Do you want to see a photo of** [4]_____?
  這裡有一些比爾和泰瑞莎的照片，你想要看他們的照片嗎？

Practice

1

請依據事實，用右邊列表的句型來回答問題。

I like him/her/them/it
I don't like him/her/them/it

1. How do you like Cristiano Ronaldo?

   I like him.

2. How do you like hiking?

   _____

3. How do you like ice cream?

   _____

4. How do you like washing clothes?

   _____

5. How do you like flowers?

   _____

6. How do you like Taylor Swift?

   _____

2

在空格處填上 me、you、him、her、it、us 或 them 來完成這篇日記。

Dear Diary,

I went to a café with my best friend tonight. Becky brought her camera and got a cute guy to take our picture. That's ❶_____ in the picture. The guy seemed to like ❷_____. After he sat down at the table with his friends, I spent a lot of time watching ❸_____. He looked back at ❹_____. Becky waved at ❺_____ and he smiled back at ❻_____. I told Becky that we should go sit with ❼_____. She liked the idea, but said we should not do ❽_____. Becky said we should make ❾_____ come and sit with ❿_____. The guy left before we could decide how to get ⓫_____ to come over. I felt like it was over for ⓬_____ and wanted to go home. So we left. I liked the café and wanted to go back again.

Unit 18

Personal Pronouns : Possessive Pronouns and Possessive Adjectives

人稱代名詞：所有格代名詞與所有格形容詞

1 所有格形容詞用來表示物品的所有權，有單數，也有複數。

單數		複數	
my	我的	our	我們的
your	你的	your	你們的
his	他的		
her	她的	their	他們的
its	它的		

Where is his car?

他的車子在哪裡？

Those are our roller blades.

那是我們的直排輪溜冰鞋。

Who is your friend?

誰是你的朋友？

2 所有格形容詞用來代替某個名詞的所有格，必須放在其他名詞前面。

I just saw Jason and his father in the park.
↳ = Jason's，放在名詞 father 前面。

我剛才在公園裡看到傑森和他爸爸。

Brenda and her twin sister are playing.
↳ = Brenda's，放在名詞 twin sister 前面。

布蘭妲和她的雙胞胎姊妹正在玩耍。

This is my lovely dog. Its name is Michael.

這是我的寶貝狗狗，牠的名字叫麥可。

• Mr. and Mrs. Smith are celebrating ___1___ twentieth wedding anniversary in a fancy restaurant.

史密斯夫婦正在一間高級餐廳慶祝他們的結婚二十週年紀念。

3 所有格代名詞用來表示物品的所有權，有單數，也有複數。

單數		複數	
mine	我的	ours	我們的
yours	你的	yours	你們的
his	他的		
hers	她的	theirs	他們的

Rita: This is my coffee. 麗塔：這是我的咖啡。
Andy: Where is mine? 安迪：那我的呢？

George and Annie have been served their food, but we are still waiting for ours.

喬治和安妮已經拿到他們的餐點，但我們的還沒拿到。

4 所有格代名詞經常用來代替已經出現過的名詞，避免重複，後面不加名詞。

Where's my mug? Is this mine?
↳ 代替已經出現過的 my mug。

我的馬克杯呢？這是我的嗎？

I found my coat. Where is yours?
↳ = your coat，避免重複 coat。

我找到我的外套了，你的呢？

These are our tickets. Did you bring yours? 這是我們的票，你們的有帶來嗎？

Isn't this a family party? We brought our whole family. Where is theirs?

這不是家庭派對嗎？我們全家都來了，他們家的人呢？

• This isn't Sam's mobile phone. ___2___ is black. 這不是山姆的手機，他的是黑色的。

• This is our bus stop. What's ___3___? 我們要在這站下車，你的站呢？

5 所有格代名詞也可以視為一個完整的名詞片語，單獨存在。

A Are these ours? 這些是我們的嗎？
B Yes, these are yours.
是的，這些是你們的。

Practice

1

一對兄妹的媽媽正在做簡短的家庭介紹。請在空格處填上 my、your、his、her、our 或 their，幫她完成這段簡介。

1. _____ name is Jane. My husband is Jerry.
2. These are _____ two kids, Jimmy and Sara.
3. Jimmy is eight years old. Those are _____ trains and cars.
4. Sara is six years old. Those are _____ dolls and stuffed animals.
5. They don't play with _____ blocks anymore.
6. Jimmy and Sara don't like cleaning up _____ room.
7. _____ house is usually a mess, but today it is clean.
8. I made Jimmy pick up _____ side and Sara cleaned up _____ side of _____ room.

2

請依圖示，在空格處填上「所有格代名詞」或「所有格形容詞」，完成句子。

Dad: Amy, it's not _____ doll. It's Nancy's doll.
Amy: I'm sorry. I didn't know it's _____ (= her doll). I'll give it back to her.

Joe: Have you seen _____ dog? I can't find it anywhere. It's a Shiba Inu.
May: No, I haven't seen _____ dog.

Jessica: Is this _____ watch?
Nick: Yes, that's _____ (= my watch).

The cat is playing _____ toy.

Mr. Anderson, that's not your office. _____ (= your office) is down there.

Unit 19

Indefinite Pronouns and Adjectives:
Some, Any

不定代名詞與不定形容詞：Some、Any

1 不定代名詞用來指**不確定、未知的人或事物**。不定代名詞有很多種。

- some 一些
- something 某物
- any 任何
- somebody 某人
- few 一些
- anyone 任何人
- one 一個
- nothing 沒有事
- many 許多
- anything 任何事
- much 許多
- everywhere 到處

2 some 和 any 可以當**形容詞**，用來**形容不確定數量**的名詞。

There are some squirrels in the tree.
樹上有一些松鼠。

There aren't any squirrels in the tree.
樹上沒有任何松鼠。

Are there any squirrels in the tree?
樹上有松鼠嗎？

3 some 和 any 可以接**複數名詞或不可數名詞**。

複數名詞

some apples 一些蘋果
any apples 任何蘋果

some carrots
一些胡蘿蔔
any carrots
任何胡蘿蔔

不可數名詞

some beer 一些啤酒
any beer 任何啤酒

some wine 一些酒
any wine 任何酒

4 some 通常用於**肯定句**，any 則用於**否定句**和**疑問句**。

We have some rice, but we <u>don't</u> have any soft drinks. 我們有一點白飯，但是沒有飲料。

<u>Are there</u> any potato chips in the cabinet?
櫃子裡有洋芋片嗎？

- I need ¹ _____ help. 我需要幫助。
- Jack doesn't want to make ² _____ mistakes. 傑克不想犯錯。
- Do you have ³ _____ cameras?
  你有相機嗎？

5 如果疑問句是屬於**禮貌性的詢問**，希望得到**肯定**的答案，那就可以用 some。

Could I have some rice, please?
可以盛點飯給我嗎？

Would you like some rice?
你要不要吃點飯？

6 若已**清楚知道所指名詞**為何，some 和 any 後面接的名詞**可以省略**，也就是把 some 跟 any 當作**代名詞**使用。

Linda: He is selling lottery tickets. Would you like some (lottery tickets)?
Bob: No, I don't want any (lottery tickets).

琳達：他正在賣樂透彩，你要買一些嗎？
鮑伯：不，我不想買。

7 若需要特別加強語氣，可用 no 來替代 not any。另外，否定詞出現在句首時，通常會用 no 來替代 not any。

There isn't any room in the car.
= There is no room in the car.
車上沒位子了。

There isn't any time. = There is no time.
我們沒時間了。

No one likes his new hairstyle.
沒人喜歡他的新髮型。

Practice

1　冰箱裡有什麼、沒有什麼？依據圖示，自表中選出適當的句型造句。

> There's some . . .
> There are some . . .
> There isn't any . . .
> There aren't any . . .

 eggs
1. *There aren't any eggs.*

 bottled water
4. _____

 meat
2. _____

 vegetables
5. _____

 **ice**
3. _____

 milk
6. _____

2　利用括號內的字，改寫右列的否定句。

* 注意：have / has got是英式句型。美式不用這種句型。

1. There isn't any space.　(no)　→ _____
2. We've got no newspapers.　(any)　→ _____
3. She hasn't got any money.　(no)　→ _____
4. There are no boxes.　(any)　→ _____
5. I've got no blank disks.　(any)　→ _____
6. He has no bonus points.　(any)　→ _____

3　用 **some**、**any** 或 **no** 填空，完成句子。

1 Would you like _____ cookies?

2 Could I have _____ bread, please?

3 There isn't _____ tea.

4 Can I have _____ nuts, please?

5 Hurry up! I've got _____ time.

6 Have you got _____ chocolate chip ice cream?

Indefinite Pronouns and Adjectives :
Many, Much, A Lot of, Enough

不定代名詞與不定形容詞：Many、Much、A Lot of、Enough

1 much、many 和 a lot of 用來表示東西的數量很多，經常當**形容詞**使用。much 用於**不可數名詞**。

A How **much** dirt is on the rug?
地毯上有多少灰塵？

B There isn't **much** dirt. 不太多。

How **much** money does it cost?
這要多少錢？

▲much dirt

2 many 用於**複數可數名詞**。

A How **many** stones are on the floor? 地板上有多少石頭？

B There aren't **many** stones.
沒有很多石頭。

▲many stones

How **many** card games do you know?
你知道幾種紙牌遊戲？

3 一般對話中，**肯定句**通常用 a lot of 或 lots of 來表示「東西的數量很多」。可用於**不可數名詞**，也可用於**複數可數名詞**。

There's a lot of **juice**. 有很多果汁。
There are a lot of **bottles**. 有很多瓶子。
Jimmy added lots of **black pepper to the soup**. 吉米在湯裡加了很多黑胡椒。
Sam bought lots of **guavas**.
山姆買了好多芭樂。

4 too much 和 too many 可用來表示「某件物品的數量已超過足夠的或希望的量」。

too much **homework** 太多作業
too many **projects** 太多案子

5 enough（足夠的）可用於**複數可數名詞**，也可用於**不可數名詞**。

I can't paint the house. I don't have enough **time**.
我沒辦法油漆這間屋子，我的時間不夠。

Do you have enough Parmesan **cheese**?
你有足夠的帕瑪森乾酪嗎？

We have enough paint **brushes**. We don't need any more.
我們已經有足夠的油漆刷子，不需要更多了。

6 用 enough 表「**足夠的數量**」，是一個固定量的最低限度；a lot of 則代表「**較大的數量**」，是一個固定量的最大限度。

enough **tea** 足夠的茶	⟷	a lot of **tea** 很多茶
enough **apples** 足夠的蘋果	⟷	a lot of **apples** 很多蘋果

7 much、many、a lot 和 enough 都可以**單獨存在**，指涉之前所指的名詞。也就是作**代名詞**用。

There's some pressure, but not much.
壓力是有一點，但是不太大。
↳ = much pressure

We have some magazines, but not a lot.
我們有一些雜誌，但是不多。
↳ = a lot of magazines

We don't need any tissues. We've got enough. 我們不用面紙，我們有的已經夠了。
↳ = enough tissues

▲ enough tissues　　▲ too many tissues

Practice

1

假設你在右列電器與相
關用品部門工作，你會
如何詢問顧客的需求？
自下表選出適當詞彙，
依照範例句型造句。

air conditioners
cell phone batteries
detergent
cameras
light bulbs
televisions
water filters

1. Video Equipment 影音設備部
   → *How many televisions do you want?*

2. Telecommunications 電信通訊部
   → _____

3. Cameras and Accessories 攝影器材部
   → _____

4. Washing Machines and Accessories 洗衣機及相關用品部
   → _____

5. Lighting 照明器材部
   → _____

6. Heating and Cooling 冷暖器材部
   → _____

7. Water Treatment 水處理設備部門
   → _____

2 用 too much、too many 和 enough 描述圖中人物平常的消費習慣。

1 He eats _____ junk food.

2 She buys _____ clothing.

3 He has _____ video games.

4 She has _____ teddy bears.

5 She eats _____ dessert.

6 She watches _____ TV.

7 She doesn't have _____ money for the toy she wants.

Unit **21**

Indefinite Pronouns and Adjectives:
Little, A Little, Few, A Few

不定代名詞與不定形容詞：
Little、A Little、Few、A Few

1 little、a little、few、a few 都是用來
表示**數量**的代名詞兼形容詞。

little **food** 沒什麼食物

a little **sugar** 少許糖

few **things** 沒多少事

a few **cups** 幾個杯子

2 a little 和 a few 的意思都是「一點
點」，a little 用於**不可數名詞**，a few
用於**複數可數名詞**。

We have a little **food** and a few **soft
drinks.** 我們有一些食物和一些飲料。

We have lots of spaghetti, but only
a little **sauce** and just a few **meatballs.**
我們有很多義大利麵，但卻只有一點醬汁
和一些肉丸。

- There is ¹ _____ seaweed in the
  tank.
  魚缸裡有一些水草。

- I have ² _____ English novels.
  Do you want to read one?
  我有幾本英文小說，你要看嗎？

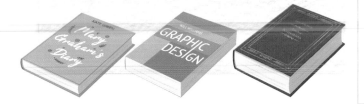

3 little 和 few 的意思是「**幾乎沒有**」，
little 用於**不可數名詞**，few 用於**複數
可數名詞**。

There are few **people** she likes.
She loves only herself.
她沒有什麼喜歡的人。
她只愛她自己。

Jack got little **help**
from his brother.
傑克的哥哥沒有
幫他什麼忙。

- She is arrogant, and ³ _____
  people like her. (few)
- There is ⁴ _____ traffic in some
  rural areas. (little)

4 little、a little、few、a few 都可**單獨
存在**，指涉之前所指的名詞。也就是當
作**代名詞**使用。

Few **of us** can speak German.
我們沒幾個人會說德文。

Only a few **of the students** agreed to
participate in the charity event on
Sunday.
只有少數學生願意參與週日的慈善活動。

Ted drank a little of the wine on the
table, so there is little left.
泰德喝了一些桌上的酒，所以所剩無多了。

5 much 是 little 的反義字；
many 則是 few 的反義字。

much **tea**	⟷	little **tea**
很多茶		沒有什麼茶
many **apples**	⟷	few **apples**
很多蘋果		沒有幾個蘋果

Practice

1

依照圖示，描述相關物品的數量。你可以從下表挑出最適當的用語，完成句子。

> There are a few . . .
> There are a lot of . . .
> There are many . . .
> There isn't much . . .
> There's a little . . .
> There's a lot of . . .

1 ▶ bananas

There are a lot of bananas.

2 ▶ books

....

3 ▶ masks

....
....

4 ▶ beer

....
....

5 ▶ sandwiches

....
....

6 ▶ gift boxes

....
....

7 ▶ candles

....
....

8 ▶ passion fruit

....
....

2

依據圖示，用下表詞彙完成右列段落。

> little
> a little
> few
> a few
> much
> many
> a lot of

There is not ❶.......................... furniture in this room. There are only ❷.......................... chairs and a cushion. ❸.......................... dirt can be found on the floor. The curtains are open, and the large window allows ❹.......................... light to come into the room.

There are ❺.......................... tables and chairs in the square. It's getting dark. I think we're expecting ❻.......................... rain later, but the weather broadcast says there won't be much rain.

53

Unit 22

Indefinite Pronouns:
One, Ones, and Some Compound Pronouns

不定代名詞：

One、Ones 與一些複合代名詞

1 one 和 ones 都可以當**代名詞**，
one 替代重複出現的**可數單數名詞**；
ones 替代重複出現的**複數名詞**。

可數單數名詞   複數名詞

peanut 花生   peanuts
↓   ↓
one   ones

I am getting <u>a glass of orange juice</u>.
Do you want one?
↳ = a glass of orange juice
我要去拿一杯柳橙汁，你要嗎？

My <u>house</u> is the small one.
↳ = house
我家是小的那間。

Do you like large <u>cars</u> or small ones?
↳ = cars
你喜歡大車還是小車？

Where did you take those <u>photographs</u>,
the ones on the wall?
↳ = photographs
牆上的那些照片，你是在哪裡拍的？

2 one 和 ones 只能替代**可數名詞**。

I want to buy <u>a cup of coffee</u>. Would you
like one? 我想要買一杯咖啡，你要嗎？
↳ = a cup of coffee；單數可數名詞

We have lots of <u>snacks</u>.
Try the ones on the table.
↳ = snacks；複數可數名詞
我們有很多點心，吃吃看桌上這些吧。

3 疑問詞 which 後面可以接 one 或
ones，來表示「哪一個」或「哪
一些」。

We have lots of soft
drinks. <u>Which</u> one would
↳ = Which soft drinks
you like, Fanta, Pepsi,
or Coke?
我們有很多種軟性飲料，
你要哪一種，芬達、百事
可樂還是可口可樂？

We have many on-line games here at the
cyber café. <u>Which</u> ones do you like to
play?   ↳ = Which on-line games
我們網咖有很多線上遊戲，你想要玩哪幾種？

4 **不定代名詞**還包含了一些由 every-、
some-、any- 和 no- 四種字首所組成
的複合代名詞，可以說是代名詞中最
大的群組。（請見 Unit 23–25 詳述）

	every-	some-	any-	no-
-one	everyone	someone	anyone	no one
-body	everybody	somebody	anybody	nobody
-thing	everything	something	anything	nothing
-where	everywhere	somewhere	anywhere	nowhere

- **My desk is the** [1] _____ **on the left.**
  我的桌子是左邊的那一個。
- **These pictures are the** [2] _____ **you
  wanted.** 這些照片是你想要的那些。

Practice

1

請依照圖示，在空格填上 one 或 ones 完成對話。

1

Mother：　Sweetheart, which ＿＿＿＿＿ would you like?

Girl：　　I want the small ＿＿＿＿＿.

Mother：　Wouldn't you like the big ＿＿＿＿＿?

Girl：　　No way! That's for big girls.

2

Jane：　Which ＿＿＿＿＿ did you catch?

Joe：　I caught the little ＿＿＿＿＿.

Jane：　You should buy the large ＿＿＿＿＿ from that guy or you'll go hungry.

3

Mia：　　How much are the ＿＿＿＿＿ on the left?

Peter：　They are extremely expensive.

Mia：　　Oh. How much are the ＿＿＿＿＿ on the right?

Peter：　They are very expensive, too.

Mia：　　Do you have a cheap ＿＿＿＿＿?

Peter：　No, madam. I am sorry. We don't have any cheap ＿＿＿＿＿ in the store.

Mia：　　OK. Thanks. I guess I can't get ＿＿＿＿＿ here.

Unit 23

Indefinite Pronouns:
Someone/Somebody, Anyone/Anybody

不定代名詞：Someone / Somebody
與 Anyone / Anybody

1 somebody 和 someone 都可以代表「**不確定的人**」，兩個字的意思完全相同。

Somebody **left an umbrella.**
有人留下了一把傘。

Someone **claimed the lost umbrella.**
有人說遺失的那把傘是他的。

2 anybody 和 anyone 都可用來代表「**非特定的人**」，兩個字的意思完全相同。

Anybody **could have entered the contest.**
任何人都可以參加這場比賽。

Anyone **who enters the contest needs to pay $100.**
任何參加這場比賽的人都要繳 100 元。

I thought I saw somebody **at the door.**
我想我看見門口有個人。

I didn't see anyone **at the door.**
我沒有看見門口有任何人。

3 somebody 和 anybody 都是**單數**，作主詞用時要接**單數動詞**。如果在同一句中再次提及，要用 **he or she**。（在非正式用法中，有些人也用複數代名詞 **they** 替代，並接複數動詞。）

Somebody **should call the police, shouldn't they?**
應該有人去叫警察的，不是嗎？（非正式用語）

Anybody **messes with the kid and he or she will have to answer to me.**
誰要是敢去招惹那個小孩，我將唯他／她是問。

4 someone/somebody 和 anyone/anybody 的用法差別，和 some 與 any 的差別是一樣的。someone/somebody 通常用於**肯定句**。anyone/anybody 通常用於**否定句**和**疑問句**。

Somebody **called my private phone line.**
有人打我的專線電話。

Someone **called about delivering a package.**
有人打電話來問送包裹的事。

I never gave anybody **that phone number.**
我從未把那個電話號碼給任何人。

Hasn't anyone **delivered the package yet?**
已經有人送來包裹了嗎？

5 在**需要幫忙或支援**的狀況下，可以使用 somebody 和 someone，此時 someone 和 somebody 也可以用於**疑問句**。

Someone **will be right with you.**
馬上會有人來幫你。

Is there somebody **who can help me?**
有沒有人可以幫幫我？

6 somebody、anybody 後面若接**動詞**，需使用**不定詞**（to V）形式，不用 -ing 形式。

If there is anybody to talk **to, I'll do the talking for us.**
如果有人能夠對談，我會去為我們發聲。

I think Janet needs somebody to keep **her company.** 我覺得珍奈特需要有個人來陪。

7 somebody、anybody 是**單數**，複數則要用 some people。

Some people **are all talk and no action.**
有些人只會出一張嘴。

1

用 someone 或 anyone 填空，完成句子。

1 Helen： I saw _____ in the alley last night.

Peter： Oh?

Helen： Did you see _____ in the alley last night?

Peter： I didn't see _____ in the alley last night.

2 Ray： You don't look good. What's the matter?

Elain： I lost my job. I'm so helpless, and there isn't _____ who can help me.

Ray： There must be _____ who can help. Don't worry.

3 Jack： What is Sandy doing?

Bella： She is talking to _____ on the phone.

Jack： Is it _____ we know?

Bella： No, it's _____ we've never heard of.

4 Vincent： Amanda, I asked you not to tell _____ about my secret.

Amanda： I didn't tell _____ about it.

Vincent： Obviously, _____ besides you and me has known about it. I'm so painful. I really don't want _____ else to know.

5 Tom： _____ stole my notebook.

Kenny： Who could possibly do that?

Tom： It could be _____ in this classroom.

2

圈選正確答案。

1. Some people never **go / goes** out on the weekend.

2. Is there someone **talk / to talk** to about your problem?

3. **Someone / Anyone** mailed a box to me last week.

4. What would you do if **someone / anyone** tried to rob you in the street.

5. If **someone / anyone** sees Lisa, ask her to call me.

6. I can go by myself. I don't need anyone **to keep / keeping** me company.

7. I talked to **someone / anyone** in the personnel department about my job.

Unit **24**

Indefinite Pronouns：Something/
Somewhere, Anything/Anywhere

不定代名詞：**Something / Somewhere**
與 **Anything / Anywhere**

1 something 和 anything 都是指「不特定的狀況或事物」。

Something is wrong with my car.
我的車子有點毛病。

At this point, I am willing to try anything.
到了這個時刻，我願意做任何嘗試。

2 something 和 anything 這類的詞都是**單數**，要接**單數動詞**，在同一句中被再次提及時，也用單數代名詞 it 替代，並接**單數動詞**。

Something is walking towards us.
What is it?
有什麼東西往我們這邊走來，到底是什麼？

I will eat anything if it is good for my health.
只要對健康有益，我什麼都吃。

3 something 和 anything 的用法差別，和 some 與 any 的差別一樣。
something 通常用於**肯定句**，
anything 通常用於**否定句**和**疑問句**。

There is something in my left shoe.
我左邊鞋子裡有東西。

Is there anything wrong with you?
You look sad.
發生了什麼事嗎？你看起來很難過。

We haven't had anything to drink for two days. 我們已經連續兩天沒東西喝了。

4 somewhere、anywhere 用來指「非特定的地點場所」。

She lives somewhere in Florida.
她住在佛羅里達州的某處。

I don't want to go anywhere today.
我今天哪裡都不想去。

5 在**需要幫忙**或**支援**的狀況下，可以使用 something 和 somewhere。此時 something 和 somewhere 可以用於**疑問句**。

Is there something I can help you with while you wait?
你在等的時候需要我幫什麼忙嗎？

Is there somewhere safe in this town?
這個鎮上有哪裡是安全的嗎？

Is there somewhere we can meet?
有沒有什麼地方是我們可以碰面的？

6 如果表示「**無論什麼事**」、「**無論什麼地方**」時，anything 和 anywhere 也可以用於**肯定句**。

If you need anything, just let me know.
你如果需要任何東西，就告訴我。

My family would love to live anywhere in this city.
我們家想住在這個城市裡，哪裡都好。

We can meet anywhere.
我們到任何地方碰面都可以。

7 something、anything 後面若接動詞，需使用**不定詞**（to V）形式，不用 -ing 形式。

Ⓐ Would you like something to eat?
Ⓑ Yes, bread and milk.
Ⓐ 你想吃些什麼嗎？
Ⓑ 想吃麵包和牛奶。

There isn't anything interesting to watch on TV tonight.
今天晚上沒有什麼有趣的電視節目。

Practice

1

利用下表中的不定代名詞和動詞來完成句子。

anything
something
anywhere
somewhere

to eat
to go
to do
to drink

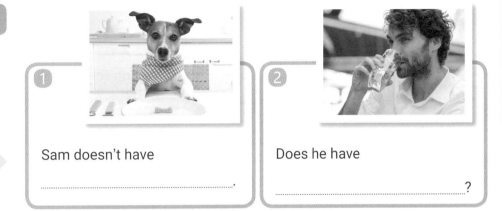

① Sam doesn't have

....

② Does he have

.... ?

③ They don't have

....

④ He still has

....

2

圈選正確答案。

1. Don : Is there **something / anything** in your drawer?

   Lee : There isn't **something / anything** in my drawer.

2. I know somewhere for us **hide / to hide**.

3. There's **something / anything** in my eye that makes me uncomfortable.

4. I want to give you **something / anything** for your birthday.

5. I can't find my passport **somewhere / anywhere**.

6. Do you have anything **to read / reading**?

7. Joe : Where did you go yesterday?

   John : I didn't go **somewhere / anywhere**.

   John : Then what did you do?

   John : I didn't do **something / anything**, either.

   Joe : Didn't you have anything **doing / to do** at all?

   John : Oh, I did do one thing. I slept all day yesterday.

Unit 25

Indefinite Pronouns: No One/Nobody/Nothing/Nowhere, Everyone/Everybody/Everything/Everywhere

不定代名詞：No One / Nobody / Nothing / Nowhere 與 Everyone / Everybody / Everything / Everywhere

1 no one / nobody / nothing / nowhere 和 everyone / everybody / everything / everywhere 都可以作
不定代名詞使用，要與**單數動詞**搭配。

I guess it was nothing important.
我想這沒什麼重要的。

We looked everywhere, but nobody was there. ↳ 注意，這個句子裡的 everywhere 是副詞的用法。
我們到處都找過了，但是那裡一個人也沒有。

Everything is under control.
一切都在掌握之中。

2 no one 和 nobody 都是「**沒有人**」的
意思，兩者意義完全一樣。

There is nobody here.
這裡一個人影也沒有。

No one came to give Ed a hand.
沒人來幫艾德的忙。

3 nobody 和 nothing 比 not anybody
和 not anything 的**語氣更強烈**。

語氣強烈	語氣和緩
Nobody can help. 完全沒有人可以幫忙。	There isn't anybody who can help. 沒有人可以幫忙。
Nothing can be added. 完全沒什麼可以補充了。	There isn't anything that can be added. 沒有什麼可以補充了。

4 nowhere 和 everywhere 用來指
「**非特定的地點場所**」，這兩個字除
了當代名詞之外，也常作**副詞**使用。

There's nowhere I can go to hide from him.
↳ 代名詞
沒有地方可以讓我躲他。

My dog follows me everywhere I go.
我走到哪我的狗就跟我到哪。 ↳ 副詞

5 no one / nobody / nothing / nowhere
後面常接**to**加不定詞格式，表示「沒有
人／沒有事／沒有地方可以……」。

There's no one to talk to.
沒有人可以跟我說話。

I have nobody to turn to for help.
我求助無門。

I have nowhere to go and nothing to do.
我沒有地方可以去，也沒有事情可做。

6 no one / nobody / nothing / nowhere
本身已經具有**否定**意味，因此在句中**不
可搭配 not 或 never** 這類的否定詞。同一
個句子中使用雙重否定是不被允許的。

~~I don't want to see nobody now.~~
I don't want to see anybody now.
我現在誰也不想見。

~~I never said nothing about this to Kenny.~~
I said nothing about this to Kenny.
我沒有對肯尼說過關於這個的事。

7 everyone 和 every one 的差別在於，
everyone 等於 **everybody**，指「**人**」；
every one 可以指人或**物**，而且一定
要**和 of 連用**（every one of . . .）。
anyone 和 any one 的區別也是一樣。

Everyone is excited about the coming event on Sunday.
人人都為即將到來的週日活動感到興奮。

Every one of us will attend the meeting.
我們都會去參加這個會議。

There isn't anyone here who speaks Chinese. 這裡沒有人會說中文。

Does any one of you play tennis?
你們有人會打網球嗎？

1

請利用括弧內的字，
改寫右列各句。

1. There isn't anybody at the office. (nobody)
   → _There is nobody at the office._

2. There isn't anyone leaving today. (no one)
   → _____

3. There isn't anything to feed the fish. (nothing)
   → _____

4. There isn't anywhere to buy envelops around here. (nowhere)
   → _____

5. There is nobody here who can speak Japanese. (anybody)
   → _____

6. There is no one that can translate your letter. (anyone)
   → _____

7. There is nothing that will change the manager's mind. (anything)
   → _____

8. There is nowhere we can go to get out of the rain. (anywhere)
   → _____

2

將右列句子改寫為
正確的句子。

1. I don't have nowhere to go.
   → _____

2. Noone believed me.
   → _____

3. Everything are ready. Let's go.
   → _____

4. There is nothing eat.
   → _____

5. I never want to hurt nobody.
   → _____

6. Every one in this room will vote for me.
   → _____

7. Did you see my glasses? I can't find it nowhere.
   → _____

8. Any one who doesn't support this idea please raise your hand.
   → _____

Unit 26

This, That, These, Those
指示代名詞與指示形容詞

1 用來指明、指定名詞的代名詞，叫做**指示代名詞**。所指的人或物若是**單數**，用 this 或 that；所指的人或物若是**複數**，則用 these 或 those。

This is Mary's coat. 這是瑪莉的大衣。

That is Jason's watch. 那是傑森的手錶。

These are my dogs. They are Michael, Big Boy, and Fifi.
這些是我的狗，牠們叫做麥可、大寶和菲菲。

Those are my mother's friends.
那些人是我媽媽的朋友。

2 當所指人或物就**在說話者附近時**，用 this 或 these 表示。當所指人或物**離說話者較遠時**，則用 that 或 those 表示。

This is Mr. Jones. He is president of the Swan Company.
這位是瓊斯先生，他是天鵝公司的董事長。

Who are those men? 那些人是誰？

3 指示代名詞 this、that、these 和 those 可以**代替所指涉的名詞**，單獨存在。

This is the book I want.
↳ =this book
這本正是我想要的書。

That is not the book I want.
↳ =that book
那本不是我想要的書。

These are the books I was looking for.
↳ =these books
這些正是我在找的書。

Those are not the books I was looking for.
↳ =those books
那些不是我在找的書。

4 this、that、these 和 those 除了作代名詞，也常作**形容詞**使用，此時後面會接**名詞**。

Look at this painting. 看看這幅畫。

Check out that sculpture. 檢查那座雕像。

I love these prints. 我喜歡這些圖片。

Let's go see those drawings.
我們去看那些畫。

5 this、that、these 和 those 也可用來表示**時間**。「正在發生的事」或「即將發生的事」用 this 或 these，「已經發生的事」用 that 或 those。

We're going camping this weekend.
我們這個週末要去露營。

I'm quite busy these days. 我這幾天很忙。

I went downtown that night.
那天晚上我進城去了。

Don't you miss those summers?
你不懷念那幾年的夏天嗎？

1

看圖用 this、that、these 或 those 填空，完成句子。

①

.... pencil is Johnny's.

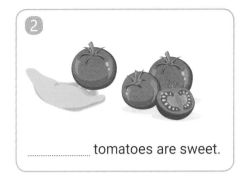

②

.... tomatoes are sweet.

③

Whose bottle water is ....?

④

.... pencil is Jenny's.

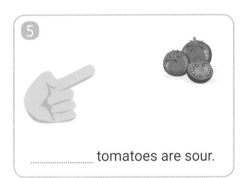

⑤

.... tomatoes are sour.

⑥

Whose earrings are ....?

2

選出正確的答案。

1. Is **this / these** the book you want?

2. Do you recognize **that / those** man in the blue shirt?

3. Does our dog love **that / those** toys?

4. What are you up to **these / those** days?

5. We had a lot of snow **that / those** year.

6. We're going to have heavy rain **this / that** year.

7. **That / Those** children are hungry.

8. Will you move **this / these** boxes for me?

9. **This / That** was the end of the vacation.

10. Schoolchildren used chalk and slate boards in **these / those** days.

Unit 27

Reflexive Pronouns and "Each Other"
反身代名詞與相互代名詞 Each Other

1 每個人稱代名詞都有一個相對應的**反身代名詞**。單數反身代名詞以 -self 結尾，複數反身代名詞則以 -selves 結尾。

	人稱代名詞		對應的反身代名詞	
單數	I	我	myself	我自己
	you	你	yourself	你自己
	he	他	himself	他自己
	she	她	herself	她自己
	it	它	itself	它自己
複數	we	我們	ourselves	我們自己
	you	你們	yourselves	你們自己
	they	他們	themselves	他們自己

2 當句中的**主詞和受詞一樣**時，就要使用反身代名詞當作受詞。

You are feeling sorry for yourself.
你在自怨自艾。

The kids built the tree house by themselves. 這群小孩們自己蓋了間樹屋。

The children are now able to dress themselves. 這些孩子現在會自己穿衣服了。

Let me introduce myself.
我來自我介紹一下吧。

My aunt is looking at herself in the mirror. 我姑姑正在看鏡中的自己。

My cat likes to lick itself.
我的貓喜歡舔自己。

3 by myself 或 by yourself 這類的反身代名詞片語，意思是**獨自**（等於 alone），並無來自於別人的幫助或參與。

I always go off by myself during lunch.
= I go places alone for lunch.
午餐時我總是自個兒出去。

Do you always eat lunch by yourself in your office?
= Do you always eat lunch alone?
你都自己在辦公室吃午餐嗎？

4 反身代名詞有**強調主詞**的作用，加強敘述的重點。

I finished the report.
我把報告完成了。

↓

I finished the report myself.
我自己把報告完成了。

My coworkers were supposed to help, but I finished the report all by myself.
我同事本來應該要幫忙，但我卻靠自己完成了這份報告。

5 **相互代名詞** each other 和反身代名詞很像，也是反指主詞，但是它表達了彼此之間互相的關係。

They are taking a picture of themselves.
她們在為她們自己拍照。

They are taking pictures of each other.
他們在幫彼此拍照。

Dogs like to sniff each other.
狗狗喜歡互相聞來聞去。

Practice

1

請看圖並填入適當的反身代名詞。

I am brushing my teeth by
...........*myself*........... .

Can you carry that box by
.... ?

This book is not going to read
....

The little boy cannot dress
....

She always eats lunch by
....

Are you going to drive
.... to the
toy store?

I guess we have to
get the food by
....

Micky and Lucky
can find food by
....

2

請用 themselves 或 each other 造句說明圖中的情況。

1. They are talking to
....

2. They are filming
....

3. They are painting the wall
by ....

Review Test of Units 16–27
單元 16–27 總複習

1 自右表選出正確的第一人稱單數代名詞填空，完成句子。
→ Unit 16, 18 重點複習

1. That's _____ notebook computer.
2. This morning _____ sent an email message to the boss.
3. The funny flash animation was _____.
4. If you see someone in the chat room named Monster, that's _____.
5. _____ computer has a wireless connection to my cellphone.
6. _____ use a bluetooth connection from my computer to my cell phone.
7. Wireless Internet access is better for _____.
8. That laser mouse is _____. It's also wireless.

| me |
| I |
| mine |
| my |

2 在空格內填入正確的人稱代名詞。
→ Unit 16, 18 重點複習

1. _____ first name is Kevin. What's _____ name?
2. My husband and _____ have two children. _____ children are John and Grace.
3. Jeanie is going out to get dinner. I am going with _____.
4. Here's a photo of _____ family. That's me on the left.
5. Winnie is in love with Arthur, but _____ doesn't love _____.
6. This is your hat. _____ can't find _____. Have _____ seen _____?
7. The Jones have _____ air conditioner on. Let's turn on _____.
8. I bought a new car. I like _____ very much.
9. My cat caught two mice. _____ is playing with _____ now.
10. Kim and Tim have moved to a new apartment. _____ new apartment is rather big. _____ really love _____.
11. Linda : Where is _____ car?

    Anne : _____ is broken.

    Linda : Then how will you go to school tomorrow?

    Anne : I don't know.

    Linda : Would you like to borrow _____?

    Anne : That would be great.

3 下列各句的空格中，應填入可數名詞、不可數名詞還是兩者皆可？
請選出正確答案填入空格內。

→ Unit 19-21 重點複習

▼ green peppers

▲ wine

1 Do you have any
<u>wine / green peppers</u> ?

▼ cookies

▲ bread

2 Please have some
....

▼ ice cubes

▲ sugar

3 There's no
....

▼ combs

▲ toothpaste

4 There isn't any
....

▼ pies

▲ candy

5 How much ....
did you get?

▼ grapes

▲ juice

6 Did you get many
.... ?

▼ goats

▲ fish

7 I saw a lot of
....

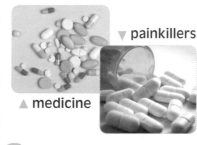

▼ painkillers

▲ medicine

8 Get me a little
....

▼ fruit tarts

▲ chocolate cakes

9 How about a few
.... ?

▼ soda

▲ soup

10 Did you get enough
.... ?

▼ leek

▲ garlic

11 How much ....
did you buy?

▼ notebooks

▲ homework

12 We have many
....

67

4 檢查各句 any 和 some 的用法是否正確。在正確的句子後寫 **OK**；
不正確的請將錯誤用字畫掉，並於句後更正。
→ **Unit 19 重點複習**

1. We have any rice. ....

2. Are there any spoons in the drawer? ....

3. There isn't some orange juice in the refrigerator. ....

4. Are there any cookies in the box? ....

5. Could I have any coffee, please? ....

6. Would you like some ham? ....

7. We have lots of fruit. Would you like any? ....

8. I already had some fruit at home. I don't need some now. ....

9. There aren't some newspapers. ....

10. There are any magazines. ....

5 請用 one 或 ones 重寫以下句子。
→ **Unit 22 重點複習**

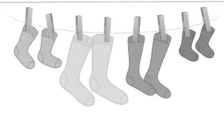

1 Who are these boxes for, the boxes you are carrying?

→ ....
....

2 Do you like the red socks or the yellow socks?

→ ....
....

3 My cubicle is the cubicle next to the manager's office.

→ ....
....
....

4 I like the pink hat. Which hat do you like?

→ ....
....
....

5 Our tennis balls are the tennis balls stored over there.

→ ....
....
....

6 選出正確的答案。

→ **Unit 20 重點複習**

1. We haven't got _____ time.

   Ⓐ many   Ⓑ much

2. We don't have _____ milk left.

   Ⓐ many   Ⓑ much

3. _____ information do you have?

   Ⓐ How many   Ⓑ How much

4. _____ people agree with you.

   Ⓐ Many   Ⓑ Much

5. He has _____ homework.

   Ⓐ too many   Ⓑ too much

6. He has _____ sandwiches.

   Ⓐ too many   Ⓑ too much

7. Do we have _____ headphones?

   Ⓐ lots of   Ⓑ little of

8. There are _____ gifts for your family.

   Ⓐ many   Ⓑ much

9. You have _____ things to do.

   Ⓐ too many   Ⓑ too much

10. Do you have _____ experience with this?

    Ⓐ many   Ⓑ much

→ Unit 23–25 重點複習

7 從下表選出適當的字首搭配標籤裡的提示字根，填空完成以下句子。

| some- | any- | no- | every- |

-where

1. I've looked for my wallet ___everywhere___, but I can't find it.

2. My wallet is _____ to be seen.

3. It must be in the house because I haven't gone _____.

4. I have to go _____, and I need my wallet.

-one

5. I called Joe's house about the party, but _____ answered.

6. Do you know if _____ is going over there tonight?

7. _____ should answer the phone.

8. _____ else intends to go there tonight except me.

-thing

9. Sue tried to tell me _____ about a problem.

10. Have you heard _____ about Sue's problem?

11. There is probably _____ I can do, but I want to help.

12. Is _____ OK with her now?

-body

13. Hello. I'm home. Hey, where is _____?

14. Is _____ home? I am here.

15. There must be _____ here because the lights are on.

16. Well, if _____ is here, then I am going to leave. Bye-bye.

8 請看圖並利用表中的不定代名詞，完成下列對話。

→ Unit 23–25 重點複習

1 **In the Musical Instrument Store**

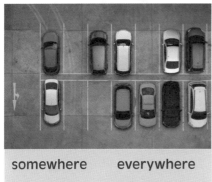

someone	anyone
no one	everyone

Woman: I am looking for ❶_____ to give opera lessons to my son.

Man: We just sell musical instruments. ❷_____ here teaches opera.

Woman: Do you know ❸_____ who teaches opera?

Man: ❹_____ likes rock and pop. ❺_____ likes opera.

Woman: Maybe my son should try gospel singing.

2 **In the Airport Parking Lot**

somewhere	everywhere
anywhere	nowhere

Woman: Your car is ❻_____ close by, right?

Man: I think so, but it could be ❼_____ in the parking lot.

Woman: It's ❽_____ to be seen. That's for sure.

Man: We haven't looked ❾_____. It could be ❿_____ else.

Woman: You keep looking. I am waiting here.

3 **In the Principal's Office at School**

something	everything
anything	nothing

Woman: You must have done ⓫_____ wrong for your teacher to send you to the office.

Boy: I didn't do ⓬_____.

Woman: Are you sure there was ⓭_____ going on?

Boy: The teacher blames ⓮_____ on me.

9 選出正確的答案。
→ Unit 26 重點複習

.... 1. .... is not my cell phone. That is mine.

       Ⓐ This   Ⓑ That   Ⓒ These

.... 2. We are going to the beach .... weekend. Would you like to join us?

       Ⓐ this   Ⓑ that   Ⓒ these

.... 3. Can you pass .... glasses to me?

       Ⓐ this   Ⓑ that   Ⓒ those

.... 4. Can you pass .... bottle of black pepper to me?

       Ⓐ this   Ⓑ that   Ⓒ those

.... 5. We had a lot of fun on .... Christmas.

       Ⓐ this   Ⓑ that   Ⓒ those

.... 6. .... suitcase belongs to Heather.

       Ⓐ This   Ⓑ These   Ⓒ Those

10 下列各句若正確，在句後寫上 OK。若句子有誤，畫掉錯誤的字並寫出
正確的反身代名詞或 each other。
→ Unit 27 重點複習

1. My brother made himself sick by eating too much ice cream. ....

2. My sister made himself sick by eating two big pizzas. ....

3. The dog is scratching itself. ....

4. I jog every morning by me. ....

5. You have only yourself to blame. ....

6. We would have gone there us but we didn't have time. ....

7. He can't possibly lift that sofa all by himself. ....

8. Do you want to finish this project by yourself or do you need help? ....

9. I helped him. He helped me. We helped ourselves. ....

10. Don't fight about it. You two need to talk to each other if you are going to solve this
problem. ....

11 選出正確的答案。
→ **Unit 19-21 重點複習**

1. I have **a little** / **a few** business to do here.

2. You need to give **a few** / **a little** examples in your essay.

3. Let's not start now. I don't have **enough** / **a little** time.

4. He has **a lot of** / **many** courage.

5. Don't buy more food. We have **many** / **enough**.

6. Buy some new clothes, but not **a lot** / **much**.

7. There is **little** / **few** we could do.

8. **Little** / **Few** people would have done as much as you did.

9. There is **enough** / **few** salad for everybody.

10. He bought **much** / **many** games.

11. You had **a few** / **a little** telephone calls.

12. There are **a lot of** / **much** boxes in the garage.

13. There were **too many** / **too much** people in line.

14. I checked the batteries. We have **enough** / **much**.

Unit 29

Present Tenses of the Verb "Be"
Be 動詞的現在時態

1 am、is、are 是表示現在時態的 be 動詞，用於**現在簡單式**和**現在進行式**。

My name is Yuki. 我名叫 Yuki。

This is my friend Akiko.
他是我朋友 Akiko。

Are you both Japanese?
你們兩個都是日本人嗎？

No, we aren't. I'm Japanese.
Akiko is Canadian.
不是，我是日本人，Akiko 是加拿大人。

2 am 只和代名詞 I 搭配使用。

I am a student. I am learning English.
我是學生，我正在學英語。

I'm not home. 我不在家。

3 **單數名詞**以及**代名詞** he、she、it 則搭配 is 使用。

The knife is very sharp. 這把刀很利。

She is a shy girl. 她是個害羞的女孩。

4 **複數名詞**以及代名詞 we、you、they 要和 are 搭配使用。

These cups are dirty. 這些杯子很髒。

We are both Chinese.
我們兩個都是中國人。

Are you interested in Chinese literature?
你對中國文學有興趣嗎？

They are just like their father.
他們跟他們父親簡直一個樣。

肯定句的全形和縮寫		否定句的全形和縮寫	
I am	I'm	I am not	I'm not
you are	you're	you are not	you aren't
he is	he's	he is not	he isn't
she is	she's	she is not	she isn't
it is	it's	it is not	it isn't
we are	we're	we are not	we aren't
they are	they're	they are not	they aren't

疑問句的句型	肯定和否定簡答的句型	
Am I . . . ?	Yes, I am.	No, I'm not.
Are you . . . ?	Yes, you are.	No, you aren't.
Is he . . . ?	Yes, he is.	No, he isn't.
Is she . . . ?	Yes, she is.	No, she isn't.
Is it . . . ?	Yes, it is.	No, it isn't.
Are we . . . ?	Yes, we are.	No, we aren't.
Are they . . . ?	Yes, they are.	No, they aren't.

5 wh 疑問詞通常搭配 is 使用。

搭配疑問詞的 全形和縮寫	
who is	who's
what is	what's
when is	when's
where is	where's
why is	why's
how is	how's

Where is my backpack?
我的背包在哪裡？

How is everything?
一切還順利嗎？

Who is the man next to Will?
威爾旁邊那個人是誰？

Practice

1

利用 be 動詞的現在時態（am、is 或 are）填空，完成右列段落。

My name ❶_____ Eizo. I ❷_____ the singer in a band called the Rockets. My best friend ❸_____ Haruki, and he ❹_____ the guitar player. Ichiro ❺_____ the bass player. Kiyonobu ❻_____ the drummer. Ichiro and Kinonobu ❼_____ brothers. We ❽_____ a rock band. I ❾_____ trying to get the band a gig playing at a pub. The place ❿_____ called the Beer Bar. We ⓫_____ not making enough money from our music, so we ⓬_____ all working day jobs. That ⓭_____ the life of a musician. We ⓮_____ used to it.

2

請依你的真實情況，填上 am、am not、is、isn't、are 或 aren't。

1. I _____ Taiwanese.
2. I _____ a student.
3. I _____ working.
4. My favorite subject _____ English.
5. My only two languages _____ Chinese and English.
6. My main interest _____ business.
7. There _____ lots of job openings in my area.
8. Language skills _____ helpful.

3

依照提示和範例，描述圖中人物的國籍和職業。

| 1 Karl | 2 Dominique | 3 Hiroko |

Italian
American
Japanese
French
Canadian
Chinese

drummer
policeman
businessman
chef
violinist
singer

Karl is Canadian. _____

He is a violinist. _____

| 4 Lino | 5 Jane | 6 Mike |

_____

_____

Unit 30

There Is, There Are

有……

---

1 there is 和 there are 用來表示
「可以看到或聽到某物的存在」。

There's **a clock on the wall.** 牆上有個時鐘。

There's **a spider** in the bathroom.
浴室裡有一隻蜘蛛。

There are **ants** in the kitchen.
廚房裡有螞蟻。

there 搭配 be 動詞的全形和縮寫	
there is	there's
there is not	there isn't
there are	there're
there are not	there aren't

2 這種句型裡，真正的主詞位於 be 動詞
後面。
be 動詞後面的主詞若為**不可數名詞**或
單數可數名詞，則使用 there is 的句
型。
主詞若是**物品**，再次提及這個主詞時
可用 it 來代替。

There's **an umbrella in the hall.** It's in the
closet.   ↳ 指走廊的
那把傘。
走廊有一把傘，就在櫃子裡。

There's **a phone call for Jane.** It's her
friend Katie.   ↳ 指打電話的人。
有一通電話找珍，是她朋友凱蒂打來的。

There isn't **any time** left.
沒有時間了。   ↳ 不可數名詞 time 要搭配
there is 或 there isn't 使用。

3 be 動詞後面的主詞若為**複數可數名
詞**，則使用 there are 的句型。再次
提及這個主詞時可用 **they** 來代替。

There are **some pens in the living room.**
They're in the drawer under the phone.
↳ 指客廳裡的那些筆。
客廳裡有一些筆，就在電話下的抽屜裡。

There are **several letters for you.**
They're on your desk.
↳ 指那些信件。
你有一些信，它們就放在你的書桌上。

• There are some glasses on the table, but
    ¹_____ not clean.
桌上有一些杯子，但是都不乾淨。

4 將 be 動詞移到句首，就構成了
疑問句。

Steve: Is there **a broom in the closet?**
Susan: No, **there isn't.**
史帝夫：櫥櫃裡有掃把嗎？
蘇珊：   沒有。

Ted: Are there **any kangaroos in the
        zoo?**
Ann: No, **there aren't.**
泰德：   動物園有沒有袋鼠？
安：   沒有。

• There is a dictionary on the shelf.
    ²_____ David's.
架上有一本字典，那本字典是大衛的。

Practice

1

依據圖示，並使用下表提供的文字，完成右列句子。

| there is |
| there isn't |
| there are |
| there aren't |

1. _____ any broccoli on the top shelf.
2. _____ some tomatoes on the bottom shelf.
3. _____ any meat in the refrigerator.
4. _____ a lot of grapes in the refrigerator.
5. _____ still some room on the shelves of the refrigerator door.
6. _____ a bottle of mineral water on the bottom shelf of the refrigerator door.
7. _____ some cheese on the top shelf.
8. _____ a carton of milk on the bottom shelf of the refrigerator door.
9. _____ any chicken in the refrigerator.
10. _____ some grapes on the bottom shelf.
11. _____ any apple on the bottom shelf.
12. _____ two oranges.
13. _____ three guavas.
14. _____ some watermelon.
15. _____ any milk on the bottom shelf.
16. _____ some vegetables on the bottom shelf.

2

用下列詞彙完成句子。

| is |
| isn't |
| are |
| aren't |
| it is |
| they are |
| it |
| them |

1. There _____ some orange juice. _____ in the refrigerator.
2. There _____ any rice wine in the kitchen. Can you go buy some? You can buy _____ at the grocery store on Tenth Street.
3. There _____ a bottle of mouth wash in the bathroom. _____ beside the sink.
4. There _____ many stray dogs in the streets. _____ very hungry.
5. There _____ some fantastic programs on TV this weekend. _____ on Channel 6.
6. There _____ a lot of homework tonight. _____ too much.

Part 3 Present Tenses 現在時態

Unit 31

Have Got
「擁有」的說法：Have Got

1 have got 和 has got 只能用於**現在式**，是 have 和 has 比較不正式的說法，兩者意思相同。
但have / has got 主要用於英式，美式用 have / has 表示「**擁有**」。

I have got a new boyfriend. 英式
= I have a new boyfriend.
我有一個新男友。

He has got blue eyes.
= He has blue eyes.
他有一雙藍色的眼睛。

I've got an extra pencil. You can use it.
我有多一支鉛筆，你可以用。

2 have got 和 has got 的**疑問句**，是把 have 和 has 移到**句首**。不能加助動詞 do 或 does。

Tim: Have **you** got a pencil, Sam?
Sam: No, I have only got an eraser.
提姆：山姆，你有沒有鉛筆？
山姆：沒有，我只有橡皮擦。

Has **she** got blonde hair?
= Does she have blonde hair?
她有一頭金髮嗎？

3 回答 have got 或 has got 的問句時，若採用**簡答**，不能用 have got、has got 或 haven't got、hasn't got，而要用 have、has 或 haven't、hasn't。

Josh: Has **your wife** got a job?
Tom: Yes, she has.
　　　　　↳ 不能用 Yes, she has got.
喬許：你老婆有工作嗎？
湯姆：有，她有。

Jason: Have **you** got a cellphone?
Helen: No, I haven't.
　　　　　↳ 不能用 No, she hasn't got.
傑森：你有手機嗎？
海倫：我沒有。

肯定句的全形和縮寫	
I have got	I've got
you have got	you've got
he has got	he's got
she has got	she's got
it has got	it's got
we have got	we've got
they have got	they've got

否定句的全形和縮寫	
I have not got	I haven't got
you have not got	you haven't got
he has not got	he hasn't got
she has not got	she hasn't got
it has not got	it hasn't got
we have not got	we haven't got
they have not got	they haven't got

疑問句的句型	
Have I got . . . ?	Has it got . . . ?
Have you got . . . ?	Have we got . . . ?
Has he got . . . ?	Have they got . . . ?
Has she got . . . ?	

肯定和否定的簡答方式	
Yes, I have.	No, I haven't.
Yes, you have.	No, you haven't.
Yes, he has.	No, he hasn't.
Yes, she has.	No, she hasn't.
Yes, it has.	No, it hasn't.
Yes, we have.	No, we haven't.
Yes, they have.	No, they haven't.

Practice

1

根據圖示，找出相符的寵物名，並利用下表的句型造句。

- hamster
- pig
- cat
- snake
- dog
- parrot

She's got a hamster.

_____

_____

_____

_____

2

利用 have / has got 和題目所提供的詞彙，寫出問句。

1. your family / cottage on Lake Michigan

....

2. you / your own room

....

3. you / your own closet

....

4. How many cups / you

....

5. How many TVs / your family

....

6. How many cars / your brother

....

Part 3 Present Tenses 現在時態

Unit 32

Present Simple Tense
現在簡單式

1 時態是用來表達某個**動作進行的時間和狀態**的動詞形式。以時間來看,可分為**現在式、過去式和未來式**。

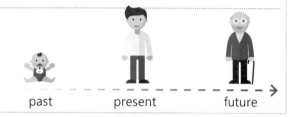

past　　　　present　　　　future

2 現在簡單式用來表示**習慣**以及**重複發生的事**,經常和一些**頻率副詞**搭配使用。

I often eat squid. 我常吃烏賊。
I rarely eat meat. 我很少吃肉。
Peggy drinks coffee every day.
珮琪每天喝咖啡。

常用的頻率副詞:
① every day 每天
② usually 通常
③ often 經常
④ sometimes 有時
⑤ never 從不
⑥ yearly 一年一次
⑦ rarely 鮮少

3 現在簡單式的構成,如果主詞是**第一人稱代名詞 I、第二人稱代名詞 you** 或者**複數名詞**,就使用**動詞原形**。

I cook dinner every Thursday.
我每個星期四都會做晚餐。

My grandparents like oatmeal.
我的祖父母喜歡燕麥粥。

4 若主詞是**第三人稱單數名詞或代名詞**,則動詞則要使用加了s、es或ies的第三人稱單數動詞形式。
　　大多數動詞在字尾加s;字尾是s、ch、sh、x、z、o的動詞,加上es;字尾是**子音+ y**的動詞,刪除y,加ies。

Joe reads a book every day.
喬每天看書。

She sometimes goes jogging in the evening.
她有時傍晚會去慢跑。

The baby cries every night.
這嬰兒每晚哭鬧。

5 現在簡單式否定句的構成,如果主詞是**複數名詞或者代名詞 I、you、we、they**,就在句中加上 do not 或 don't;如果主詞是**第三人稱單數名詞或代名詞**,就在句中加上 does not 或 doesn't。

My wife doesn't cook dinner on Thursdays.
我太太星期四都不做晚餐。

They don't play tennis.
他們不打網球的。

I don't wash dishes.
我不洗碗的。

6 現在簡單式的疑問句,是在句首加上 do 或 does,並且動詞使用原形。
回答也是用 do 或 does 來構成簡答。

Eve:　Do you like cereal and milk for breakfast?
依芙:　你早餐喜歡吃牛奶麥片嗎?
Bob:　I do. 鮑伯:　喜歡。
Jude:　Does Wendy drive to work every day?
裘德:　溫蒂每天開車上班嗎?
Sid:　Yes, she does. 席德:　是的。

否定句的全形和縮寫		疑問句的句型	肯定和否定的簡答方式	
I do not	I don't	Do I . . . ?	Yes, I do.	No, I don't.
you do not	you don't	Do you . . . ?	Yes, you do.	No, you don't.
he does not	he doesn't	Does he . . . ?	Yes, he does.	No, he doesn't.
she does not	she doesn't	Does she . . . ?	Yes, she does.	No, she doesn't.
it does not	it doesn't	Does it . . . ?	Yes, it does.	No, it doesn't.
we do not	we don't	Do we . . . ?	Yes, we do.	No, we don't.
they do not	they don't	Do they . . . ?	Yes, they do.	No, they don't.

Practice

1

請寫出右列動詞的第三人稱單數動詞。

1. eat _____
2. drink _____
3. walk _____
4. run _____
5. paint _____
6. bury _____
7. watch _____
8. carry _____
9. unbox _____
10. crunch _____
11. try _____
12. chase _____
13. cut _____
14. go _____
15. fix _____
16. teach _____

2

右列是 Bobby 和 Jenny 日常行程的描述，請分辨其中哪些動詞是「現在簡單式」，將它們畫上底線。

Bobby ▶ I cook simple food every day. I usually heat food in the microwave oven. I often make sandwiches. I sometimes pour hot water on fast noodles. However, I don't wash dishes.

Jenny ▶ I usually get up at 6:00 in the morning. I eat breakfast at 6:30. I leave my house at 7:00. I walk to the bus stop. I take the 7:15 bus. I always get to work at 8:00. I have lunch at 12:30. I leave work at 5:30. I take the bus home. I arrive at my home about 6:30. I eat dinner at 7:00. I often fall asleep after the 11:00 news ends.

3

現在簡單式經常可以用來說明工具的功能。請依據圖示，自下表選用適當的動詞，用「現在簡單式」造句說明每個工具的功能。

cut
move
tighten
push
pound
make

1. A saw _____ wood.

2. A wrench _____ bolts.

3. A drill _____ holes.

4. A cart _____ boxes.

5. A hammer _____ nails into wood.

6. A bulldozer _____ earth and stones.

Unit 33

Present Continuous Tense
現在進行式

1 現在進行式用來表示現在**持續不斷**或正在進行的動作，由「be 動詞 + V-ing」所構成。

I'm making a strawberry cake.
我正在做草莓蛋糕。

The sun is rising. 旭日正在升起。

Little Susie and Pinky are playing with their dolls. 小蘇西和蘋綺正在玩洋娃娃。

- It ¹ _____. 現在正在下雨。
- Watson ² _____ a novel.
  華生正在讀小說。

Rick is putting a jigsaw puzzle together.
瑞克正在玩拼圖。

2 動詞的**進行式**是在字尾加上 ing，變化方式如下：

❶ 直接加上 ing。
clean → cleaning
清掃
study → studying
研讀
walk → walking 走路

❷ 字尾是 e 的動詞，去掉 e 再加 ing。
bake → baking 烘焙
rise → rising 升起
hope → hoping 希望

❸ 字尾是 ie 的動詞，把 ie 改成 y，再加 ing。
die → dying 死亡
lie → lying 說謊
tie → tying 捆

❹ 字尾是「單母音 + 單子音」的動詞，重複字尾子音，再加 ing。
stop → stopping 停止
hit → hitting 打

3 現在進行式的疑問句，只要將 be 動詞移到句首。

May: Hello? What are you doing?
Victor: I am watching TV.
May: Are you doing your homework?
Victor: Yes, I am. This is for the TV class.

梅： 哈囉！你在做什麼？
維多： 我在看電視。
梅： 你在做功課嗎？
維多： 對啊，這是電視廣播課的作業。

- ³ _____ you ⁴ _____ English now?
  你在唸英文嗎？
- ⁵ _____ he ⁶ _____ in the pool now? 他正在池子裡游泳嗎？

肯定句的全形和縮寫	
I am thinking	I'm thinking
you are thinking	you're thinking
he is thinking	he's thinking
she is thinking	she's thinking
it is thinking	it's thinking
we are thinking	we're thinking
they are thinking	they're thinking

否定句的全形和縮寫	
I am not thinking	I'm not thinking
you are not thinking	you aren't thinking
he is not thinking	he isn't thinking
she is not thinking	she isn't thinking
it is not thinking	it isn't thinking
we are not thinking	we aren't thinking
they are not thinking	they aren't thinking

疑問句的句型	
Am I thinking . . . ?	Is it thinking . . . ?
Are you thinking . . . ?	Are we thinking . . . ?
Is he thinking . . . ?	Are they thinking . . . ?
Is she thinking . . . ?	

肯定和否定的簡答方式	
Yes, I am.	No, I'm not.
Yes, you are.	No, you aren't.
Yes, he is.	No, he isn't.
Yes, she is.	No, she isn't.
Yes, it is.	No, it isn't.
Yes, we are.	No, we aren't.
Yes, they are.	No, they aren't.

Practice

1

將右列動詞，加上 ing，並根據規則做必要的變化。

1. talk _____
2. care _____
3. stay _____
4. sleep _____
5. jog _____
6. eat _____
7. make _____
8. rob _____
9. advise _____
10. die _____

11. spit _____
12. stare _____
13. wait _____
14. clip _____
15. swim _____
16. cry _____
17. lie _____
18. plan _____
19. throw _____
20. speak _____

2

請依圖示，自下表選出適當的動詞，以「現在進行式」完成句子。

lie

walk

buy

run

picnic

sit

play

shine

eat

1. The girl _____ a dog.
2. The woman _____ fruits.
3. The sun _____.
4. The cat _____ with a ribbon.
5. The girls _____.
6. A surfboard _____ on the beach.
7. They _____.
8. The girl _____ ice cream.
9. Mike _____ on the lifeguard chair.

Unit 34

Comparison Between
the Present Continuous Tense
and the Present Simple Tense
現在進行式和現在簡單式用法比較

1 現在進行式用來**描述說話當下正在發生的事**，或**詢問某人當下正在做什麼**。句子裡經常會出現 now 或 right now 這樣的詞。

Leslie is in the warehouse now. She's making an inventory.
雷思莉在倉庫裡，她正在開一張存貨清單。

Where is Leslie? Is she working in the warehouse?
雷思莉在哪裡？她在倉庫裡工作嗎？

2 現在簡單式用來描述一再重複的事情，與講話當下的狀況並無緊密關連。句子裡經常會出現 every day、usually、often、sometimes 這些頻率副詞。

Ian checks his email every day.
伊恩每天都會收電子郵件。

Does Ivana often update her blog?
伊凡娜有經常更新她的部落格嗎？

3 讓我們用同樣的動詞來比較看看。

現在進行式

I'm listening now. Please say it.
我正在聽，請說。

Stop, thief! He's stealing my bicycle.
站住，小偷！他正在偷我的腳踏車。

現在簡單式

I usually listen to heavy metal rock music.
我通常都聽重金屬搖滾樂。

He frequently steals things, and sooner or later he will get caught and put into jail.
他慣性地偷竊，遲早會被抓去關的。

4 問句中，「What are you doing?」用來詢問對方正在做什麼事；「What do you do?」則用來詢問一個人的**工作或職業**。

Jay：What are you doing?
Kay：I'm playing a computer game.
Jay：What do you do?
Kay：I am a computer game designer.

杰：你在做什麼？
凱：我正在玩電腦遊戲。
杰：你是做什麼的？
凱：我是電腦遊戲的設計師。

比較

Sarah is a freelance writer. She writes for several newspapers and magazines. She works hard for over 8 hours a day. Right now she is working on his computer. She is writing a story about a wind farm in Mongolia.

莎拉是一名自由作家。她為幾家報紙及雜誌寫文章。她一天認真工作超過八小時。她現在正在電腦前工作，寫一篇關於蒙古風力農場的報導。

比較

Jamie is a computer security specialist. He works for a computer security firm. He protects corporate data networks. He is watching a hacker trying to break into a computer right now. He is trying to stop the hacker at the moment.

傑米是一名電腦安全防禦專家，他在一家電腦防禦公司上班，負責保護公司的資料網。他現在正盯著一名試圖入侵的駭客，試著阻止他。

1

自字彙表選出適當的動詞，並正確使用現在簡單式或現在進行式，填空完成句子。

| leave | drive | wish | drink | end | think | design | go |

Bob Jones is stuck in traffic. He's ❶_____ to work. Every day he ❷_____ at 8:00 in the morning. He is a microwave engineer. He ❸_____ communication systems for mobile phone operators. Whenever he ❹_____ up sitting in a traffic jam, he ❺_____ some coffee and listens to music. Right now he ❻_____ about how fast microwaves travel and how slow he ❼_____ in the traffic jam. He ❽_____ he were a speedy little microwave.

2

判斷以下句子應使用現在簡單式或現在進行式，利用題目提供的詞彙，組合造問句，根據事實做出簡答之後，再寫出完整的句子描述事實。

| 主詞 | 頻率副詞 | 動詞片語／形容詞 |

1. | you | often | listen to music |

Ⓠ _Do you often listen to music?_
Ⓐ _Yes, I do. I often listen to music._

2. | you | at this moment | watch TV |

Ⓠ _____
Ⓐ _____

3. | it | now | hot |

Ⓠ _____
Ⓐ _____

4. | it | often / this time of year | hot |

Ⓠ _____
Ⓐ _____

5. | you | every day | drink coffee |

Ⓠ _____
Ⓐ _____

6. | you | right now | drink tea |

Ⓠ _____
Ⓐ _____

Unit 35

Verbs not Normally Used in
the Continuous Tense
通常不能用進行式的動詞

1 下列動詞，通常不會用於進行式，會
用於**現在簡單式**（或**過去簡單式**）。

want	想要	I want a notebook.
believe	相信	I believe in you.
belong to	屬於	This bag belongs to you.
forget	忘記	I forget things easily.
hate	恨	I hate you.
know	知道	I know the answer.
like	喜歡	Dogs like meat.
mean	意指	I mean what I say.
need	需要	I need a dictionary.
own	擁有	Jack owns a sports car.
prefer	寧願	I prefer fish.
realize	瞭解	Do you realize how difficult it will be?
recognize	認識	I don't recognize you.
remember	記得	He remembers everything.
seem	似乎	You seem tired.
understand	瞭解	I understand you.

Can you understand our waiter? He has a funny accent. 你懂我們服務生的意思嗎？
他有一種奇怪的口音。

2 有些字不只一個意思。當它用於某種
意思時，不能用進行式。
動詞 think 表示「**用腦子想**」的時
候，可以用**進行式**；表示「**相信／認
為**」時，就只能用**簡單式**。

Give me a minute. I'm thinking. 思考
給我一分鐘，我正在想。

I think I will try a cinnamon raisin scone.
我想我會試試肉桂葡萄乾司康餅。認為

3 動詞 have/has 不只一種意思：
當它表示「**吃**」的動作時，可以用**進
行式**；當它表示「**擁有**」時，就只能
用**簡單式**。

Julie is having breakfast at the café.
↳ 表「吃」，可用進行式。
茱麗正在咖啡廳吃早餐。

Lily has a cottage by Deer Lake.
↳ 表「有」，用簡單式。
莉莉在鹿湖旁有一間小屋。

4 has got 和 have got 的意思是
「**擁有**」，只能用於**現在簡單式**。

Yvonne has got two sisters and three brothers. 伊芳有兩個姊妹和三個兄弟。

We have got a new house. 我們有個新家。

5 一些**感官動詞**應使用**簡單式**，
或者加上 can，而不用進行式。

smell 聞   hear 聽

see 看   taste 嚐

I can smell something burning in the kitchen. 我聞到廚房裡有燒焦的味道。

I can see him coming this way.
我看到他往這裡走來。

This soup tastes delicious.
這湯很好喝。

Can you hear the man talking?
你聽得到那個人說話嗎？

Practice

1

請用「現在簡單式」或「現在進行式」，填空完成右列句子。

1. I _____ (eat) stewed prunes, but I really _____ (hate) stewed prunes.

2. Harry _____ (eat) a banana.

   He _____ (like) bananas.

3. Ron _____ (love) his weekend hiking trips.

4. The Jameson family _____ (like) to barbeque.

5. Jack and Jane _____ (make) sushi right now.

   They _____ (know) how to make sushi.

6. _____ you _____ (mean) we can leave now?

7. You _____ (seem) very tired. What _____ you _____ (do) right now?

8. _____ you _____ (go) to Sam's house?

   _____ you _____ (need) a ride?

9. Lucy _____ (carry) a backpack. This backpack _____ (belong) to her.

10. _____ you _____ (understand) what the teacher is saying?

11. John _____ (remember) to deliver a pot of chicken soup to his grandma every Saturday morning.

2

右列句子，若動詞的用法正確，請在句後寫上OK；若錯誤，請刪掉錯誤的用法並更正。

1. I am owning my own house. _____

2. This book belongs to Mary. _____

3. Mother is believing your story. _____

4. I often forget names. _____

5. I am having a snack. _____

6. The man is recognizing you. _____

7. The story is needing an ending. _____

8. You are seeming a little uncomfortable. _____

9. Are you feeling sick? _____

10. Do you have got a swimsuit? _____

Unit 36 Review Test of Units 29–35
單元 29–35 總複習

1 寫出下列動詞的「第三人稱現在式」和「現在進行式」。

→ Unit 32, 33 重點複習

1. change *changes* *changing*		11. tie
2. visit		12. apply
3. turn		13. jump
4. jog		14. enjoy
5. mix		15. steal
6. cry		16. swim
7. have		17. send
8. cut		18. taste
9. fight		19. finish
10. feel		20. study

2 請用 is 或 are 以及題目所提供的字造問句；並根據事實回答。

→ Unit 29 重點複習

1. What / your favorite TV show

   Q *What is your favorite TV show?*

   A *The Simpsons.*

2. What / your favorite movie

   Q

   A

3. Who / your favorite actor

   Q

   A

4. Who / your favorite actress

   Q

   A

5. What / your favorite food

   Q

   A

6. What / your favorite juice

Q ....

A ....

7. Who / your parents

Q ....

A ....

8. Who / your brothers and sisters

Q ....

A ....

3 參考圖片回答問題。先用 **is** 或 **are** 完成問句,再依事實回答問題。

→ **Unit 29 重點複習**

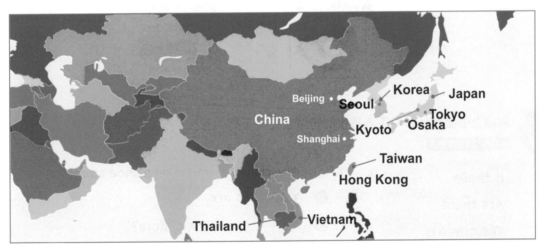

1. Q _Is_ Seoul in Vietnam?

   A _No, Seoul is in Korea._

2. Q .... Thailand and Vietnam in East Asia?

   A ....

3. Q .... Hong Kong in Japan?

   A ....

4. Q .... Beijing and Shanghai in China?

   A ....

5. Q .... Osaka in Taiwan?

   A ....

6. Q .... Tokyo, Osaka, and Kyoto in Japan?

   A ....

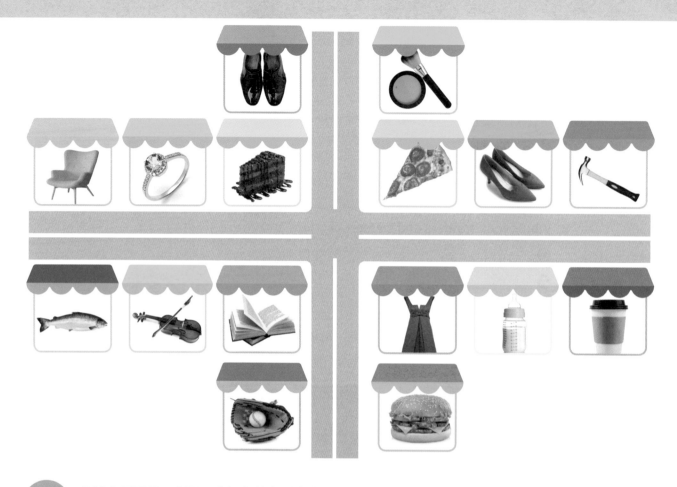

4 依據上面圖示，利用下表提供的句型來完成下列問答。

→ Unit 29 重點複習

Is there
Are there
Yes, there is.
No, there isn't.
Yes, there are.
No, there aren't.

1. Q ____Are there____ any men's shoe stores?
   A ____Yes, there are.____

2. Q _____ a wig store?
   A _____

3. Q _____ a computer store?
   A _____

4. Q _____ two bookstores?
   A _____

5. Q _____ any women's clothing stores?
   A _____

6. Q _____ any women's shoe stores?
   A _____

7. Q _____ three music stores?
   A _____

8. Q _____ a jewelry store?
   A _____

5 請正確填上 am、are、is、have 或 has。
→ Unit 29-31 重點複習

1. My name _____ Leo.
2. I _____ a security guard at a bank.
3. I _____ got a gun.
4. There _____n't any bullets in my gun.
5. If the bank _____ a problem, I call the police.
6. Uh oh! There _____ two bank robbers.

7. I _____ moving closer to the robbers.
8. They _____ reaching out to grab something.
9. Hands up! Oops! I made a mistake. They _____ vice presidents.
10. I _____ sorry. I made a mistake.

6 請用 is 或 are 以及題目所提供的字造問句；並根據事實，以肯定或否定句型簡答。
→ Unit 29 重點複習

1. you / university student

   Q *Are you a university student?*

   A *Yes, I am. / No, I'm not.*

2. you / big reader

   Q

   A

3. your birthday / coming soon

   Q

   A

4. your favorite holiday / Chinese New Year

   Q

   A

7 看圖用 there is 或 there are 來描述圖中有什麼物品。
→ Unit 30 重點複習

1. *There is an alarm clock on the dresser.*
2.
3.
4.
5.

8 用 do、does、don't、doesn't 和 work、works，填空完成句子。
→ Unit 32 重點複習

Jasmine: ❶＿＿＿＿＿ you ❷＿＿＿＿＿ or go to school?

Anthone: I ❸＿＿＿＿＿ go to school. I ❹＿＿＿＿＿ at a bank.

Jasmine: ❺＿＿＿＿＿ your friend George ❻＿＿＿＿＿ too?

Jasmine: Yes, he ❼＿＿＿＿＿ at the same bank as I do.

Jasmine: ❽＿＿＿＿＿ he ❾＿＿＿＿＿ in the same department as you do?

Anthone: No, he ❿＿＿＿＿. I ⓫＿＿＿＿＿ in the trust department.

He ⓬＿＿＿＿＿ in the foreign exchange department.

9 用 do 或 does 以及題目所提供的詞彙造問句，再依真實的情況簡答，
並寫出完整句子描述事實。
→ Unit 32 重點複習

1. you / watch many movies

   Ⓠ＿＿＿＿＿＿＿＿＿＿＿＿＿＿＿＿＿＿＿＿＿＿＿＿＿＿＿＿＿＿＿＿

   Ⓐ＿＿＿＿＿＿＿＿＿＿＿＿＿＿＿＿＿＿＿＿＿＿＿＿＿＿＿＿＿＿＿＿

2. your mother / work

   Ⓠ＿＿＿＿＿＿＿＿＿＿＿＿＿＿＿＿＿＿＿＿＿＿＿＿＿＿＿＿＿＿＿＿

   Ⓐ＿＿＿＿＿＿＿＿＿＿＿＿＿＿＿＿＿＿＿＿＿＿＿＿＿＿＿＿＿＿＿＿

3. your father / drive a car to work

   Ⓠ＿＿＿＿＿＿＿＿＿＿＿＿＿＿＿＿＿＿＿＿＿＿＿＿＿＿＿＿＿＿＿＿

   Ⓐ＿＿＿＿＿＿＿＿＿＿＿＿＿＿＿＿＿＿＿＿＿＿＿＿＿＿＿＿＿＿＿＿

4. your family / have a big house

   Ⓠ＿＿＿＿＿＿＿＿＿＿＿＿＿＿＿＿＿＿＿＿＿＿＿＿＿＿＿＿＿＿＿＿

   Ⓐ＿＿＿＿＿＿＿＿＿＿＿＿＿＿＿＿＿＿＿＿＿＿＿＿＿＿＿＿＿＿＿＿

5. your neighbors / have children

   Ⓠ＿＿＿＿＿＿＿＿＿＿＿＿＿＿＿＿＿＿＿＿＿＿＿＿＿＿＿＿＿＿＿＿

   Ⓐ＿＿＿＿＿＿＿＿＿＿＿＿＿＿＿＿＿＿＿＿＿＿＿＿＿＿＿＿＿＿＿＿

6. you / have a university degree

   Ⓠ＿＿＿＿＿＿＿＿＿＿＿＿＿＿＿＿＿＿＿＿＿＿＿＿＿＿＿＿＿＿＿＿

   Ⓐ＿＿＿＿＿＿＿＿＿＿＿＿＿＿＿＿＿＿＿＿＿＿＿＿＿＿＿＿＿＿＿＿

10 閱讀 Annabelle 的自我介紹，並從字彙表選出適當的詞彙，造問句詢問她問題。

→ Unit 32 重點複習

Hi, my name is Annabelle, but I like my friends to call me Annie. I am from Singapore. I am working at a junior high school in Hong Kong. After school at 4:00 I usually go to my favorite café. I have a cup of black coffee, read a newspaper, and grade some papers. About 6:00, I take the bus home, have dinner, and watch TV. I go to bed early because I have to get up early. I have to be at school by 6:45 a.m. During the school year I am busy every day.

| go home |
| go home |
| come from |
| like to be called |
| drink at the café |
| have to be at school |
| go to the café |

1. What _do you like to be called_ ?

2. Where _____ ?

3. What time _____ ?

4. What _____ ?

5. What time _____ ?

6. How _____ ?

7. What time _____ ?

11 用 have got 或 has got 改寫下列句子，若不能改寫，則畫上✕。

→ Unit 31 重點複習

1. Peter has a good car.

   → _____

2. Paul is having a haircut right now.

   → _____

   _____

3. Wendy has a brother and a sister.

   → _____

4. The Hamiltons have two cars.

   → _____

5. Ken has a lot of good ideas.

   → _____

   _____

6. My sister is having dinner with her friend right now.

   → _____

   _____

7. I have the answer sheet.

   → _____

12 請依圖示，自字彙表選出適當的動詞，以現在進行式完成句子。

→ **Unit 32 重點複習**

deliver

use

fix

change

talk

work

1. Sam .... the suspension.

2. Peter .... packages.

3. Joe .... the tire.

4. Bill .... on the phone.

5. Chuck and Debbie .... the computer.

6. They .... in the computer industry.

13 選出正確的答案。

→ **Unit 33–35 重點複習**

1. **I am going / I go** to the store now.

2. I usually **stop / stopping** at the store on my way home from work.

3. Frank is working at the store. **He often has / He's often having** the afternoon shift.

4. The store **is having / is having got** a big sale on diapers.

5. Frank **wants / is wanting** a break from selling baby supplies.

6. Frank is taking a break now. He **is having / has** some cookies and a glass of milk.

7. "Be quiet," Frank says to Joe. "**I'm thinking / I think** about something."

8. "**I have got / I am having** an idea," says Frank.

9. "**I don't believe / I'm not believing** you," says Joe.

10. "You're not thinking. **I can hear / I'm hearing** you snoring."

14 請將下列句子改成否定句和疑問句。

→ **Unit 29–33 重點複習**

1. We're tired.

→ ....

→ ....

2. You're rich.

→ ....

→ ....

3. There's a message for Jim.

→ ....

→ ....

4. It is a surprise.

→ ....

→ ....

5. They have got tickets.

→ ....

→ ....

6. You have got electric power.

→ ....

→ ....

7. She works out at the gym.

→ ....

→ ....

8. He usually drinks a fitness shake for breakfast.

→ ....

→ ....

9. We are playing baseball this weekend.

→ ....

→ ....

10. He realizes this is the end of the vacation.

→ ....

→ ....

Unit **37**

Past Tenses of the Verb "Be"
Be 動詞的過去時態

1 was 和 were 是表示**過去時態**的 be 動詞，用來表示「**過去的某一狀況**」。也可以當作助動詞，與述語動詞的 -ing 形式一起構成**過去進行式**，表示「過去某時刻正在發生的事」。

I was on vacation last month.
I wasn't on sick leave.
我上個月是去度假，不是請病假。

Sam and Susie were in Berlin for a week.
山姆和蘇西在柏林待了一個禮拜。

It was raining all day yesterday.
昨天下了一整天的雨。

2 主詞如果是**單數名詞**，或者是**代名詞** I、he、she、it，be 動詞則要用 was。

| I was | he was | she was | it was |

I was at home last night.
我昨天整晚都在家。

It was so much fun at the electronic music festival. 參加電子音樂節非常好玩。

Vicky was a law student for six years.
薇琪念了六年的法律。

- I ¹ _____ in town yesterday.
  我昨天在鎮上。
- Janet and Mother ² _____ employed at the JJ Company for two years.
  珍奈特和媽媽曾經在 JJ 公司工作了兩年。
- It ³ _____ snowing last night.
  昨晚一直下雪。
- They ⁴ _____ not happy on the trip to Bali last month.
  他們上個月去峇里島玩得不太愉快。

否定句的全形和縮寫	
I was not	I wasn't
you were not	you weren't
he was not	he wasn't
she was not	she wasn't
it was not	it wasn't
we were not	we weren't
they were not	they weren't

疑問句的句型	
Was I . . . ?	Was it . . . ?
Were you . . . ?	Were we . . . ?
Was he . . . ?	Were they . . . ?
Was she . . . ?	

肯定和否定簡答的句型	
Yes, I was.	No, I wasn't.
Yes, you were.	No, you weren't.
Yes, he was.	No, he wasn't.
Yes, she was.	No, she wasn't.
Yes, it was.	No, it wasn't.
Yes, we were.	No, we weren't.
Yes, they were.	No, they weren't.

3 主詞如果是**複數名詞**，或者是**代名詞** you、we、they，be 動詞則要用 were。

| you were | we were | they were |

Page: Were you and your friend in Berlin for the electronic music festival?

Craig: Yes, we were.

佩吉： 那時你和你朋友在柏林參加電子音樂節嗎？

克雷格：對啊。

They were not in school yesterday.
他們昨天不在學校裡。

Practice

1

請判斷句中的時態，自下表選用正確的 be 動詞完成句子。

| is |
| are |
| was |
| were |

1. Laura _____ a medical student for a long time. Now, she _____ a doctor.
2. Tammy _____ a cute little girl, and now she _____ a beautiful woman.
3. Today _____ a rainy day. Yesterday _____ a rainy day, too.
4. Today _____ January 1st, so yesterday _____ December 31st.
5. That _____ a big dog, but once it _____ a puppy.
6. Fluffy _____ such a busy little kitty, but now she _____ a lazy old cat.
7. The grapes _____ OK yesterday, but today they _____ overly ripe.
8. The new recruits _____ in Boot Camp last month. Now they _____ in technical school.
9. The thieves _____ in jail now. Last year they _____ not in jail.
10. We _____ so upset when we heard the news, but now we _____ feeling better.
11. Musicals _____ very popular in the past, and they _____ still popular today.
12. At one time, cell phones _____ uncommon, but now they _____ everywhere.

2

用 was 或 were 完成右列問句，依照實際情形做出簡答，並寫出完整句子描述事實。

1. _____Were_____ you busy yesterday?
   → _Yes, I was. I was very busy yesterday._
2. _____ you at school yesterday morning?
   → _____
3. _____ yesterday the busiest day of the week?
   → _____
4. _____ your father in the office last night?
   → _____
5. _____ you at your friend's house last Saturday?
   → _____
6. _____ your mother at home at 8 o'clock yesterday morning?
   → _____
7. _____ you in bed at 11 o'clock last night?
   → _____
8. _____ you at the bookstore at 6 o'clock yesterday evening?
   → _____

Past Simple Tense (1)
過去簡單式（1）

1 過去簡單式可用來表示「**過去曾經存在或發生過的事**」。這件事可以是短暫的單一事件，也可以是持續性或反覆發生的事件。

Stella called a cab. The cab drove her home.
史黛拉叫了一輛計程車。計程車載她回家。

Kelly: I went to Paris on vacation.
Sean: Did your boyfriend Andrew go?
Kelly: Andrew didn't go with me.
Sean: Did you go alone?
Kelly: No, I didn't. I went with my new boyfriend, Henry.

凱莉：我去了一趟巴黎度假。
席恩：你的男友安德魯有一起去嗎？
凱莉：安德魯沒有和我一起去。
席恩：那你是一個人去的囉？
凱莉：不是，我和我的新男友亨瑞一起去。

2 過去簡單式經常和一些表示**過去時間**的**副詞**搭配使用。

I walked to the mall yesterday.
昨天我走路去購物中心。

Thomas Edison invented a lot of devices in the 19th century.
愛迪生於十九世紀發明了許多裝置。

表示過去時間的副詞：
① yesterday 昨天
② last week 上週
③ last month 上個月
④ in 2005 在 2005 年
⑤ in the 20th century 在二十世紀

3 **過去簡單式**的動詞要使用過去式動詞，其中**規則動詞**的過去式是在**字尾加上** ed。規則如下：

❶ 直接加上 **ed**。
visit → visited 參觀
wash → washed 洗
play → played 玩耍

❷ 字尾是 **e** 的動詞只加 **d**。
love → loved 愛
dance → danced 跳舞
hate → hated 恨

❸ 字尾是「**子音 +y**」的動詞，去掉 y，再加 ied。
study → studied 研讀
fry → fried 油炸
copy → copied 影印

❹ 字尾是「**單母音 + 單子音**」的單音節動詞，重複字尾子音，再加 ed。
jog → jogged 慢跑
nod → nodded 點頭

規則動詞發音規則

規則動詞的過去式，字尾 ed 有 /ɪd/、/d/ 和 /t/ 三種發音，規則如下：
❶ 動詞字尾發**無聲子音** /f/、/k/、/p/ 時，ed 的讀音為 /t/。
 · jumped /dʒʌmpt/ 跳 · laughed /læft/ 笑
❷ 動詞字尾發**有聲子音**或**母音**時，ed 讀音為 /d/。
 · skimmed /skɪmd/ 撇過
 · towed /toʊd/ 拖拉
❸ 動詞字尾發 **/t/** 或 **/d/** 的音時，ed 的讀音為 /ɪd/。
 · visited /ˈvɪzɪtɪd/ 參觀
 · needed /ˈnidɪd/ 需要

4 **不規則動詞**的過去式，請一一記下它們的拼寫。

go → went 走
buy → bought 買
tell → told 告訴
make → made 做
run → ran 跑
get → got 拿取
choose → chose 選擇
hear → heard 聽到

cut → cut 切
hit → hit 打
read → read 讀
set → set 設立
cost → cost 花費
let → let 讓
put → put 放
shut → shut 關閉

Practice

1

寫出右列動詞的
過去式。

1. walk _____
2. run _____
3. cough _____
4. write _____
5. eat _____
6. drop _____
7. ask _____
8. pick _____
9. show _____
10. drink _____
11. wait _____

12. type _____
13. marry _____
14. fly _____
15. go _____
16. use _____
17. join _____
18. play _____
19. look _____
20. like _____
21. send _____
22. jog _____

2

依據圖示，自下表選
出適當的動詞，用過
去式來描述圖中人物
做過什麼。

use
attend
receive
check
count
put

1. He _____ the
   money.

2. They _____
   a meeting.

3. She _____
   some email.

4. She _____
   a photocopier.

5. He _____
   the inventory.

6. He _____ a box
   on the shelf.

Past Simple Tense (2)
過去簡單式（2）

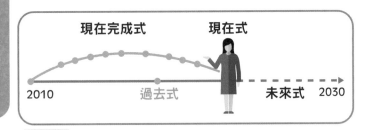

現在完成式　　現在式

2010　　　過去式　　　未來式　2030

---

1 過去簡單式的否定句，是在主詞後面使用「did not + 動詞原形」或縮寫「didn't + 動詞原形」。

I didn't mean to hurt you.
我不是故意要傷害你。

She did not arrive on time.
她並未及時趕到。

Mark and Tanya didn't go to the market yesterday morning.
馬克和譚雅昨天早上並沒有去市場。

---

2 過去簡單式的疑問句，是在句首加上 Did，**動詞**也要使用原形。

Did you call me this morning?
你今天早上有打電話找我嗎？

Did you lock Mr. Jones in his room?
你把瓊斯先生鎖在房間裡嗎？

Did your brother stay up late last night?
你哥哥昨晚是不是熬夜？

肯定簡答的句型，都是用「主詞 + did.」。
否定簡答的句型，都是用「主詞 + didn't」。

- Yes, I did.
- No, I didn't.

過去簡單式經常用來說故事：

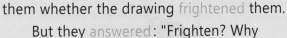

I showed my masterpiece to the grown-ups and asked them whether the drawing frightened them.

But they answered: "Frighten? Why should anyone be frightened by a hat?"

My drawing was not a picture of a hat. It was a picture of a boa constrictor digesting an elephant. But since the grown-ups were not able to understand it, I made another drawing: I drew the inside of the boa constrictor so that the grown-ups could see it clearly.

我把我的大作拿給大人們看，問他們這畫嚇不嚇人。他們卻回答：「嚇人？一頂帽子有什麼好嚇人的？」我畫的可不是什麼帽子，是一條大蟒蛇正在消化牠肚裡的一頭大象。好吧，既然大人們看不懂這張圖，我又畫了一張：我把大蟒蛇肚子裡的東西也畫出來，這下大人們就看得懂了。

「過去簡單式」和「現在簡單式」的比較

I am on vacation. I am in London now. Last night I went to the Tower of London. Last year I visited Paris. Two years ago I stayed in Rome for a week. I like Rome, but I like London better. I like vacations.

我正在度假，我現在人在倫敦。昨晚我去了倫敦塔。去年我去巴黎參觀，兩年前則在羅馬待了一週。我喜歡羅馬，但更愛倫敦。我很喜歡度假。

Practice

1

用 did、didn't、have 或 had，完成右列句子。

1. Ken: _____ Harry sleep late?

   Joe: Harry _____ a late night, and he _____ to get up early, so he slept late.

2. Mia: _____ you _____ a lot of phone calls last night?

   Zoe: Yes, I _____. Every time I put my head on the pillow the phone rang.

3. Bob: When _____ you _____ the time to read the book?

   Bell: I read it on the airplane. I _____ it with me on my trip.

2

用 did 和題目提供的詞彙造問句，依照實際情況做出簡答，並寫出完整句子來描述事實。

1. you　see your friends last night

   Ⓠ *Did you see your friends last night?*

   Ⓐ *No, I didn't. I didn't see my friends last night.*

2. you　go to a movie last weekend

   Ⓠ _____

   Ⓐ _____

3. you　play basketball yesterday

   Ⓠ _____

   Ⓐ _____

4. you　graduate from university last year

   Ⓠ _____

   Ⓐ _____

5. you　move out of your parents' house last month

   Ⓠ _____

   Ⓐ _____

3

用過去式改寫括弧內的動詞，完成《小王子》的部分內容。

Once when I ❶_____ (be) six years old I ❷_____ (see) a magnificent picture in a book, called True Stories from Nature, about the primeval forest. It ❸_____ (be) a picture of a boa constrictor in the act of swallowing an animal. Here is a copy of the drawing.

. . .

I ❹_____ (ponder) deeply, then, over the adventures of the jungle. And after some work with a colored pencil I ❺_____ (succeed) in making my first drawing. My drawing Number One. It looked like this:

Unit **40**

Past Continuous Tense
過去進行式

1 過去進行式用來表「**過去某一時刻正在進行的事**」。

I was watching a vampire movie from 8:00 to 12:00 last night.

past   present

昨晚 8 點到 12 點之間，我在看一部吸血鬼的電影。

否定句的全形和縮寫	
I was not watching	I wasn't watching
you were not watching	you weren't watching
he was not watching	he wasn't watching
she was not watching	she wasn't watching
it was not watching	it wasn't watching
we were not watching	we weren't watching
they were not watching	they weren't watching

疑問句的句型	
Was I watching . . . ?	Was it watching . . . ?
Were you watching . . . ?	Were we watching . . . ?
Was he watching . . . ?	Were they watching . . . ?
Was she watching . . . ?	

肯定和否定簡答的句型	
Yes, I was.	No, I wasn't.
Yes, you were.	No, you weren't.
Yes, he was.	No, he wasn't.
Yes, she was.	No, she wasn't.
Yes, it was.	No, it wasn't.
Yes, we were.	No, we weren't.
Yes, they were.	No, they weren't.

2 **過去進行式**由「be 動詞過去式 + V-ing」所構成。

What were you doing at 8:00 last night?
昨晚 8 點你在做什麼？

At 8:00 last night I was watching the news. It was a slow news day. The newscasters were talking about turtles. They were saying the sea turtles swim thousands of kilometers. It was boring so I turned off the TV.
昨晚 8 點，我正在看新聞。那天的新聞很無聊，當時播報員正在談論烏龜。他們介紹海龜可以游數千公里，這則新聞真是無趣，所以我就把電視關了。

「過去簡單式」和「過去進行式」的比較

❶ 過去進行式和過去簡單式經常連用，以**過去簡單式**描述某個動作，並以**過去進行式**描述該動作發生時的背景。

I was watching the movie when you called.
你打電話來的時候，我正在看電影。

❷ when 的後面可以用過去進行式也可以用過去簡單式，如果是**較短暫的動作**，就用**簡單式**，較長時間的動作就用**進行式**。

I called when the movie started.
電影開始播放後，我就打了電話。

The phone rang when he was taking a bath.
他在泡澡的時候，電話響了。

Practice

1

將括弧內的動詞以「過去進行式」填空。

We ❶_____ (decorate) Debbie's apartment for her surprise birthday party when the door opened. Everybody froze. Trisha ❷_____ (hang) balloons. Francine ❸_____ (drape) streamers. Annabelle ❹_____ (arrange) the forks and plates for the cake. Julie ❺_____ (put) candles on the birthday cake. Gina ❻_____ (unpack) presents from the shopping bags. Cathy ❼_____ (put) a bow and ribbon on Debbie's cat. Everybody looked at Debbie coming through the doorway. Debbie had arrived from work early. She walked in, looked around, and said, "Surprise! What are you doing?" I said, "We are preparing your surprise birthday party. Now go back outside and then come in so we can yell "Surprise! Happy birthday!"

2

用動詞「do 的過去進行式」完成問句，詢問圖中人物在做什麼。

再依據圖示，自下表選出適當的動詞片語，用「過去進行式」造句回答問題。

talk on the phone

drink coffee

sleep soundly

Ⓠ *What was she doing* when the phone rang?

Ⓐ *She was sleeping soundly.*

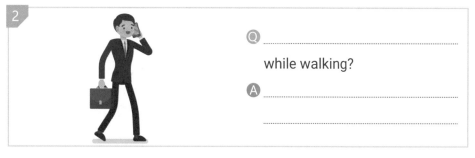

Ⓠ _____ while walking?

Ⓐ _____

Ⓠ _____ while watching TV during breakfast?

Ⓐ _____

Unit 41

Present Perfect Simple (1)
簡單現在完成式（1）

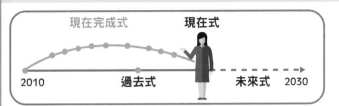

現在完成式　　　現在式

2010　　　過去式　　　未來式　2030

3 規則動詞的過去分詞和過去式同形；
不規則動詞的過去分詞必須逐一牢記。

不規則動詞

原形	過去式	過去分詞	
go	went	gone	走
buy	bought	bought	買
fall	fell	fallen	落下
rise	rose	risen	升起
build	built	built	建立
see	saw	seen	看見
write	wrote	written	寫

1 簡單現在完成式經常被視為過去時態
的一種，用來表示「**發生於過去，一直持續到現在的動作或事情**」。

We have lived here since 2005.
從 2005 年起，我們就一直住在這裡。

past
2005

moved to the house

2006

2007

2008

2009

2010

present　　still living in the house

2 現在完成式的動詞是由「have/has +
動詞的過去分詞」所構成。

We have watched all her movies.
↳ 我們對她的每一部電影都熟悉了。
我們已經看過她所有的電影。

**We haven't missed her TV show even
once.** ↳ 她的電視節目我們還是每一次都看。
她的電視節目我們一次也沒錯過。

**He has been to the library three times
today.** 他今天已經去圖書館三次了。

肯定句的全形和縮寫	
I have visited	I've visited
you have visited	you've visited
he has visited	he's visited
she has visited	she's visited
it has visited	it's visited
we have visited	we've visited
they have visited	they've visited

否定句的全形和縮寫	
I have not visited	I haven't visited
you have not visited	you haven't visited
he has not visited	he hasn't visited
she has not visited	she hasn't visited
it has not visited	it hasn't visited
we have not visited	we haven't visited
they have not visited	they haven't visited

疑問句的句型	
Have I visited . . . ?	Has it visited . . . ?
Have you visited . . . ?	Have we visited . . . ?
Has he visited . . . ?	Have they visited . . . ?
Has she visited . . . ?	

肯定和否定的簡答	
Yes, I have.	No, I haven't.
Yes, you have.	No, you haven't.
Yes, he has.	No, he hasn't.
Yes, she has.	No, she hasn't.
Yes, it has.	No, it hasn't.
Yes, we have.	No, we haven't.
Yes, they have.	No, they haven't.

Practice

1

寫出右列動詞的
「過去分詞」。

1. eat _____
2. see _____
3. write _____
4. go _____
5. love _____
6. come _____
7. fight _____
8. read _____
9. get _____
10. leave _____

11. bring _____
12. lend _____
13. cost _____
14. lose _____
15. hit _____
16. pay _____
17. find _____
18. take _____
19. ring _____
20. speak _____

2

從下表選出適當的動
詞，以「過去完成式」
填空，完成句子。

win
steal
arrive
teach
write
eat

1. Colonel Sanders _____ fried chicken all his life.
2. Mrs. Fredericks _____ at this school for 25 years.
3. Johnny Baxter _____ at the airport.
4. Kathy Stein _____ another first place ribbon.
5. John Newman _____ money from his friends.
6. Sidney Green _____ three books.

3

哪些動詞形式屬於
「現在完成式」？
將它們畫上底線。

Clive grew up in the country. He moved to the city in 2010. He has lived there since then.

He has worked in an Italian restaurant for a year and half.

He met his wife in the restaurant. They got married last month, and she moved in to his apartment. They have become a happy couple, but they haven't had a baby yet.

Unit **42**

Present Perfect Simple (2)
簡單現在完成式（2）

1 現在完成式常與 for（……多久）或 since（自……以來）連用，表示「事情延續的時間」。**for** 後面會接「一段時間」，**since** 後面則接「一個固定的時間點」。

We have been in line for 30 minutes.
我們已經排隊排了 30 分鐘了。

I have worked in Brazil for three years.
我已經在巴西工作了三年。

We have been here since 7:00.
我們從 7 點起就在這裡了。

2 現在完成式常與時間副詞 ever（曾經）或 never（從未）連用，表示「到現在為止已經發生或不曾發生某件事」。

Have you ever seen a movie star?
↳ 在你這一生中任何一刻
你曾經見過電影明星嗎？

I have never seen a movie star.
↳ 在我人生中從未有過
我從未見過任何一位電影明星。

3 現在完成式常與時間副詞 just（剛剛）、already（已經）或 yet（還沒）連用，來「指出或確認動作發生的時刻或狀況」。

Otto has just eaten the last cookie.
↳ 剛過不久（美式用過去簡單式：just ate）
奧圖剛把最後一塊餅乾吃掉。

We have already eaten at that restaurant.
↳ 之前（美式用過去簡單式：already ate）
我們已經在那家餐廳吃過飯了。

Ron hasn't finished eating yet.
朗恩還沒吃完。 ↳ 到目前為止

Have you finished reading the book yet?
↳ 到目前為止，注意：yet 只能用於否定句和疑問句
你把這本書看完了嗎？

4 現在完成式可用來「談論直到目前為止的人生經驗」。

Have you ever been to Hollywood?
你去過好萊塢嗎？

Kevin has been to Hollywood and Beverly Hills.
凱文去過好萊塢和比佛利山莊。

💬 比較

have been 去過
He has been to the library twice today.
↳ 他已經去過並回來了。
他今天去過圖書館兩次了。

have gone 去了
He is not at home. He has gone to the library.
↳ 他還沒回來。
他不在家，他去圖書館了。

have been 去過
Have you ever been to Brazil?
↳ 詢問對方過去的經驗。
你有去過巴西嗎？

have gone 去了
I hear Teddy has gone to Rio for Carnival.
↳ 泰迪現在人還在那裡。
我聽說泰迪到里約去參加嘉年華會了。

5 現在完成式可用來「談論一個目前可以看到結果的動作」。

Sally has gone to the movies.
↳ 結果是「She is at the movie theater.
她現在人在電影院。」
莎莉已經去看電影了。

Harriet has had dinner.
↳ 結果是「He is not hungry now.
他現在不餓。」
哈里特已經吃過晚餐。
↳ 美式用過去簡單式：Harriet had dinner.

Practice

1

請將括弧內的動詞以「現在完成式」來填空。

沒有動詞提示的空格，請填上 for 或 since。

1. I am an airplane pilot. I _____ (be) a pilot _____ I graduated from junior high school.

2. In high school I started making model airplanes. I _____ (build) model airplanes _____ 25 years.

3. I flew ultra-light airplanes _____ 8 years while I was in college.

4. I _____ (pilot) a dozen military aircraft during the time I was in the Air Force.

5. After leaving the Air Force, I _____ (work) for commercial airlines _____ over 20 years.

6. Ever since I was a kid, I _____ (dream) about going to the moon.

7. I _____ (wonder) if I will ever get to the moon, but I still have hopes.

8. _____ 2001, several companies _____ (start) to offer space tourism.

2

利用題目提供的字彙造問句，依據實際情況做出簡答，並寫出完整的句子來描述事實。

1. eat a worm

   Q *Have you ever eaten a worm?*

   A *No, I haven't. I haven't eaten a worm.*

2. be to Japan

   Q _____

   A _____

3. swim in the ocean

   Q _____

   A _____

4. cheat on an exam

   Q _____

   A _____

Unit **43**

Comparison Between the Present Perfect Simple and the Past Simple
簡單現在完成式和過去簡單式的比較

1 簡單現在完成式和過去簡單式都用來表示**之前做過的行為或狀況**。

簡單現在完成式是「已於過去完成，對現在仍有持續影響的事情」

past　2017　2018　2019　2020　present

I have owned **the car for over four years.**

↳ 用現在完成式表示「現在還擁有這輛車」。

這輛車我已經開了四年以上。

過去簡單式則是「已經結束、完成的行為或動作，與現在並無關聯」。

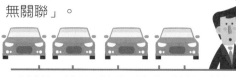

past 2016　2017　2018　2019　2020　2021 present

I owned **the car for over four years.**

↳ 用過去式表示「過去曾經擁有，但現在已經不再擁有這輛車」。

那輛車我開了四年以上。

2 現在完成式往往和 ever 或 never 連用，表達「無確切時間的過去事件或經驗」。

I have never gone **swimming in a river.**

我從未在河裡游泳過。

Have **you** ever jumped **off a three-meter diving board?**

你曾經從三公尺高的跳台跳下來嗎？

3 過去簡單式則和表達過去時間的詞彙連用，表達「有確切時間的過去事件」。

Did **you** go **to your swimming class** last Saturday? 你上星期六有去上游泳課嗎？

I went **surfing twice** last month.

我上個月衝浪兩次。

比較

- Have you ever been to a baseball game? 你去看過棒球比賽嗎？

- Did you go to the baseball game yesterday? 你昨天有去看棒球賽嗎？

4 當句子使用 when 開頭的問句，應該使用**過去簡單式**。

When did **you** pass **your scuba diving test?** 你什麼時候通過水肺潛水的測驗？

5 現在完成式代表「仍在進行中的某件事」。

過去簡單式則表「過去發生的某件事，現在已不再持續」。

Willy has gone to **Amsterdam on vacation.**　↳ 他現在人在阿姆斯特丹。

威利已經到阿姆斯特丹去度假了。

Willy went to **Amsterdam on vacation.**

　　　↳ 他現在已經從阿姆斯特丹回來了。

威利到阿姆斯特丹度過假。

Practice

1

根據圖示及內文，判斷動詞時態應該是「現在完成式」還是「過去簡單式」？

將括弧內的動詞以正確時態填入空格中。

Jimmy Jones ❶＿＿＿＿＿＿ (love) surfing since he was a teenager. He ❷＿＿＿＿＿＿ (be) to Phuket Island in Thailand six times. On his first visit in 1999, he ❸＿＿＿＿＿＿ (stay) at a popular beachfront hotel. He ❹＿＿＿＿＿＿ (go surfing) at all the beaches on the west coast. He really ❺＿＿＿＿＿＿ (like) the long white sand beaches on that side of the island. Later he ❻＿＿＿＿＿＿ (discover) cheaper hotels in Phuket City.

He ❼＿＿＿＿＿＿ (rent) a small house in the city for a month on his last trip. He ❽＿＿＿＿＿＿ (learn) how to drive a motorcycle.

He ❾＿＿＿＿＿＿ (visit) all the beaches along the southern coast.

He also ❿＿＿＿＿＿ (enjoy) fishing since he was a kid. He ⓫＿＿＿＿＿＿ (fish) all over Phuket and the outlying islands.

He last ⓬＿＿＿＿＿＿ (visit) Phuket in 2010. Since then, he ⓭＿＿＿＿＿＿ (go) to Hawaii for all of his vacations.

Recently, however, Jimmy Jones ⓮＿＿＿＿＿＿ (talk) about going back to Phuket one more time.

2

請根據上一題內容，以正確時態完成關於 **Jimmy Jones** 的問句。

1. Ⓠ How long ＿＿＿＿＿＿ a surfer?

   Ⓐ Since he was a teenager.

2. Ⓠ When ＿＿＿＿＿＿ his first trip to Phuket?

   Ⓐ His first trip was in 1999.

3. Ⓠ How many times ＿＿＿＿＿＿ to Phuket?

   Ⓐ He has been to Phuket six times.

4. Ⓠ ＿＿＿＿＿＿ to Phuket between 1999 and 2010?

   Ⓐ Yes, he did. He went to Phuket between 1999 and 2010.

5. Ⓠ ＿＿＿＿＿＿ at a beachfront hotel in 1999?

   Ⓐ Yes, he did. He stayed at a beachfront hotel in 1999.

6. Ⓠ ＿＿＿＿＿＿ all the beaches on the island since 1999?

   Ⓐ No, he hasn't visited all the beaches.

7. Ⓠ ＿＿＿＿＿＿ Jimmy Jones' last trip to Phuket?

   Ⓐ His last trip was in 2010.

1 寫出下列動詞的過去式和過去分詞。

→ **Unit 38, 41 重點複習**

1. drive
2. go
3. eat
4. write
5. think
6. keep
7. drink
8. sleep
9. make
10. stand

11. buy
12. sing
13. do
14. hide
15. fall
16. say
17. give
18. sit
19. shoot
20. teach

2 將括弧內的動詞以「過去簡單式」完成句子，並分別將句子改寫為「否定句」及「疑問句」。

→ **Unit 38, 39 重點複習**

1. I _____ (sail) on a friend's boat last weekend.

→ _____

→ _____

2. I _____ (see) a seal on the rocks.

→ _____

→ _____

3. We _____ (feed) the seagulls.

→ _____

→ _____

4. The seagull _____ (like) the bread we threw to it.

→ _____

→ _____

5. We _____ (fish) for our dinner.

→ _____

→ _____

6. My friend _____ (cook) our dinner in the galley of the boat.

→ _____

→ _____

7. We _____ (eat) on deck.

→ _____

→ _____

8. We _____ (pass) the time chatting and watching the water.

→ _____

→ _____

3 規則動詞的過去式，有 /ɪd/、/d/ 和 /t/ 三種字尾發音，請將框內單字改寫為過去式，並依照字尾發音，填至正確的欄位內。
→ Unit 38 重點複習

| start | land | fix | hike | walk | march | call | order | cart | play | hand | brush |

① _____ /d/ _____

② _____ /t/ _____

③ _____ /ɪd/ _____

4 Catherine 總是日復一日的做著同樣的事情。請閱讀以下文章，並以過去式改寫該文章的內容。
→ Unit 38-39 重點複習

Catherine gets up every morning at 5:00. She takes a shower. Then she makes a cup of strong black coffee. She sits at her computer and checks her email. She answers her email and works on her computer until 7:30. At 7:30, she eats a light breakfast. After breakfast, she goes to work. She walks to work. She buys a cup of coffee and a newspaper on her way to work. She arrives promptly at 8:30 and is ready to start her day at the office.

Catherine got up at 5:00.

5 選出正確的答案。
→ Unit 38–40 重點複習

1. It **snowed / was snowing** when I **went / was going** to bed last night.
2. After I **fell / was falling** asleep, I **had / was having** a dream.
3. We **walked / were walking** to the pet store when we **saw / were seeing** an elephant.
4. When we **saw / were seeing** the elephant, my brother John **said / was saying** he wanted to ride on it.
5. While John was riding the elephant, he **fell / was falling** off.
6. John **broke / was breaking** his glasses when he **fell / was falling** off the elephant.
7. I **fed / was feeding** the elephant when I **heard / was hearing**, "There's Jumbo."
8. When I **woke / was waking** up, I **realized / was realizing** it was only a dream.
9. As I was lying in bed, I **started / was starting** to think about going to the zoo.

6 曼果公司的銷售團隊,正在一項一項核對「應做事項表」,看看他們是否已為這次的貿易展做好了準備。經理凱莉正在和約翰和喬安這兩名業務員說話。

根據右方列表,以「現在完成式」和「have . . . yet」 的句型,造問句並做出簡答,並以「they have already . . .」或「they haven't . . . yet」的句型完整描述事實。
→ Unit 41–42 重點複習

1. ⓠ *Have they picked up the flyers yet?*
   ⓐ *Yes, they have. They have already picked up the flyers.*

2. ⓠ _____
   ⓐ _____

3. ⓠ _____
   ⓐ _____

4. ⓠ _____
   ⓐ _____

5. ⓠ _____
   ⓐ _____

6. ⓠ _____
   ⓐ _____

☑ pick up the flyers
☑ put out order pads
☐ get pens with our company logo
☑ set up the computer
☐ arrange flowers
☐ unpack boxes

7 回想你曾去過哪些地方度假？在哪一年？請依照範例，用「現在完成式 have been」的句型說出你去過的地方，再用過去式說明年分。

→ Unit 43 重點複習

1. *I have been to Tokyo. I went to Tokyo in 2008.*

2.

3.

4.

5.

6.

8 將括弧中提示的動詞，以正確的時態完成句子。

→ Unit 37–43 重點複習

1. He _____ (be) sick yesterday, but he is feeling better today.

2. Today is Monday, and Jerry is at the office. Yesterday _____ (be) Sunday, and he _____ (be) at home.

3. Lydia _____ (have) a haircut yesterday, so she has short hair now.

4. Father _____ (buy) a new shirt yesterday, and he is wearing the new shirt today.

5. Sam _____ (sleep) well last night, so he is feeling energetic today.

6. Jill and Winnie _____ (go) to Canada. They are not at home now.

7. Uncle John _____ (keep) his dog for over ten years, but it _____ (die) of old age last month.

8. He _____ (register) for this school last week.

9. Mom: _____ you _____ (finish) your homework already?

   Tim: No, I _____ (finish) it yet.

10. She _____ (cook) dinner last night when the phone rang.

11. Lily: When _____ (do) you graduate from college?

    Sunny: In 2008.

9 選出正確的答案。

→ **Unit 38–43 重點複習**

_____ 1. _____ my new computer for one year.

(A) I had　　　　(B) I've had

_____ 2. _____ my old cell phone two days ago.

(A) I've sold　　　(B) I sold

_____ 3. _____ at school last night.

(A) We've been　　(B) We were

_____ 4. The TV show _____ about 30 minutes ago.

(A) ended　　　　(B) has ended

_____ 5. When did you _____ that new hat?

(A) get　　　　　(B) got

_____ 6. _____ to Greece on vacation?

(A) Did you go　　(B) Did you went

_____ 7. Joey has worked in advertising _____ ten years.

(A) for　　　　　(B) since

_____ 8. Tommy has lived in Mumbai _____ 1995.

(A) since　　　　(B) for

_____ 9. _____ a painter since 1992.

(A) I'm　　　　　(B) I've been

Unit 45

Present Continuous for the Future
表示未來意義的現在進行式

1 現在進行式常用來表示「**未來計畫要做的行為**」，尤其是時間和地點已經確定的安排。這種用法裡，現在進行式並不具有正在進行的意味。

What is Director Nelson doing next week?
尼爾森董事下星期要做什麼？

Mon.

He is going to a board meeting on Monday.
他星期一要參加董事會議。

Tue.

He is meeting with some international customers on Tuesday.
他星期二要和國外客戶見面。

Wed.

He is flying to Moscow on Wednesday.
他星期三要飛去莫斯科。

Thu.

He is visiting an old friend in Moscow on Thursday.
他星期四要去拜訪一位住在莫斯科的老友。

Fri.

He's returning on Friday.
他星期五會回來。

2 現在進行式常用於表示「**未來之計畫、意圖、正要發生的行為**」，或是「**詢問未來的狀況**」。

I am having lunch with Ricky on Friday.
↳ 計畫
我星期五要和瑞奇一起吃午飯。

I am going for a walk. Are you coming?
↳ 正要進行的行為
我要去散步，你要來嗎？

I'm not waiting any longer.
↳ 堅決的意圖
我再也不等了。

What are you eating for lunch tomorrow? ↳ 對未來計畫的詢問
你明天午餐要吃什麼？

- I ^{1} _____ a pizza for us later tonight.
今晚晚一點我要幫我們叫一個披薩。

- Joan ^{2} _____ baseball on Saturday. 瓊恩星期六要去打棒球。

- What ^{3} _____ you ^{4} _____ next summer? 你明年夏天打算做什麼？

Practice

1

一對夫妻將要去度假。請利用圖片提供的資訊,以「現在進行式」完成問句,並回答問題。

Mark and Sharon

May 18, 2021

depart from Linz at 15:30

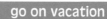
go on vacation

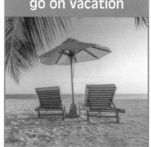

taking Aeroflot Airlines, Flight 345

arriving in Budapest at 17:30

1. Who _____*is going*_____ on vacation?

   → _Mark and Sharon are going on vacation._

2. When _____ Mark and Sharon _____ on vacation?

   → _____

3. Where _____ they _____ from?

   → _____

4. Where _____ they _____ to?

   → _____

5. What time _____ they _____ ?

   → _____

6. What time _____ they _____ at their destination?

   → _____

7. What airline _____ they _____ ?

   → _____

8. What flight _____ they _____ ?

   → _____

Unit **46**

"Be Going to" for the Future
be going to 表示未來意義的用法

肯定句的全形和縮寫	
I am going to drive	I'm going to drive
you are going to drive	you're going to drive
he is going to drive	he's going to drive
she is going to drive	she's going to drive
it is going to drive	it's going to drive
we are going to drive	we're going to drive
they are going to drive	they're going to drive

否定句的全形和縮寫	
I am not going to drive	I'm not going to drive
you are not going to drive	you aren't going to drive
he is not going to drive	he isn't going to drive
she is not going to drive	she isn't going to drive
it is not going to drive	it isn't going to drive
we are not going to drive	we aren't going to drive
they are not going to drive	they aren't going to drive

疑問句的句型	
Am I going to drive?	Is it going to drive?
Are you going to drive?	Are we going to drive?
Is he going to drive?	Are they going to drive?
Is she going to drive?	

肯定和否定的簡答	
Yes, I am.	No, I'm not.
Yes, you are.	No, you aren't.
Yes, he is.	No, he isn't.
Yes, she is.	No, she isn't.
Yes, it is.	No, it isn't.
Yes, we are.	No, we aren't.
Yes, they are.	No, they aren't.

1 be going to 常用來表示**未來**意義。

Red Riding Hood, are you going to Grandma's house **tomorrow?**
小紅帽，妳明天要去奶奶家嗎？

Yes, **Mr. Wolf,** I am going to **Grandma's house.** 沒錯，大野狼先生，我要去奶奶家。

OK, I guess I am going to **her house, too.** 很好，我想我也要去她家一趟。

2 be going to 可以用來表達「意圖」或「未來的決定」。

Are **you** going to get **a job?**
↳ 找工作的意圖
你要去找份工作嗎？
We **are** going to eat **lunch in a few minutes.**
↳ 幾分鐘內的決定
我們馬上就要吃午餐了。

· Lydia [1]
the bathroom after lunch.
莉迪雅吃完午飯後要打掃浴室。
· Lily [2] _____ Bali this summer.
莉莉今年夏天要去峇里島旅遊。

3 be going to 可表示「預測未來即將發生的事」或「無法掌握而可能發生的事」。

Be careful or **you're** going to get **hurt.**
小心點，不然你會受傷。
It looks like **we** are going to get **a visitor this evening.** 看來今晚我們可能會有訪客。
It's going to rain **at any minute.**
隨時會下雨。

4 be not going to 可用來表示「拒絕未來可能發生的事」。

I'm not going to drive **you to the shopping mall.**
我才不要載你去購物中心。

Practice

1

請依圖示，對各個疑問句做出簡答，並用完整句子描述正確情況。

1. Is Santa Claus going to use a cell phone?
   No, he isn't. He is going to use a laptop.

2. Is the woman going to buy some vegetables?

3. Is the girl going to take a nap with her teddy bear?

4. Are the grandparents going to drink some milk?

5. Are the mother and daughter going to buy some toys?

6. Is the salesperson going to give the customers a pen?

2

依據事實，用 be going to 或 be not going to 描述你今晚會不會做這些事。

1. eat at a restaurant

2. watch a baseball game

3. read a book

4. play video games

5. write an email

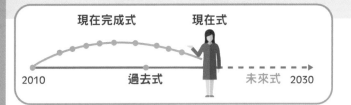

現在完成式　現在式

2010　　過去式　　未來式　2030

Simple Future Tense "Will"
未來簡單式 will

1 未來簡單式用來表示「**預測未來要發生的事情**」或是「**提供未來資訊**」或「**意圖**」。句型是「will + 動詞原形」。

意願 I will weed the garden every Saturday.
我每個星期六會除花園的草。

意圖 I will plant peas this summer.
我今年夏天要種豌豆。

2 will 通常會以縮寫「'll」的形式呈現。

She'll get married this summer.
她今年夏天要結婚了。
I'll go wherever the wedding is held.
不管婚禮在哪裡舉行，我都會去。
I'll take a pot roast out of the freezer to defrost.
我要從冰箱拿出燉牛肉來解凍。

3 will 可用來表示「**在說話時剛做的決定**」。

I think I'll have a carrot. No, wait a minute, there are no carrots left. I think I'll eat a cucumber. Oh, I already finished the cucumbers. Maybe I'll quit eating salad.
我想我要吃一根胡蘿蔔，不，等等，已經沒有胡蘿蔔了。那我吃一根小黃瓜好了。我已經吃光所有的小黃瓜了。也許我該戒沙拉了。

肯定簡答的句型，都是用「主詞 + will」。
· Yes, I will.

否定簡答的句型，都是用「主詞 + won't」。
· No, I won't.

4 will 常用來表示「**未來的生活**」。

Soon human beings will travel through space to the planets and beyond. We will live on the Moon, Mars, or maybe in another galaxy. I think I'll go to a nice little planet, not too far from my office on Earth.
很快人類就可以到外太空，甚至到更遠的星球去旅行。我們將會住在月球、火星或是其他的銀河上。我想我會選擇去一個離我地球辦公室不會太遠的美麗小行星上。

5 will 的否定是 will not，縮寫為 won't，經常用來表示「**拒絕**」、「**不願意**」。

I won't give you any money.
我不會給你錢的。
No matter what I say, Mary just won't open the door.
不論我怎麼說，瑪麗就是不開門。
I won't forget you. 我不會忘記你的。

6 will 常和 think（想）、hope（希望）、perhaps（或許）這些字搭配使用。

I think I'll eat that fish.
我想我會吃了那條魚。

I hope I will pass the exam.
我希望我會通過考試。
Perhaps he will visit his grandma this summer. 或許今夏他會去探望奶奶。
I doubt Johnny will tell the truth.
我不覺得強尼會說真話。

think 如果要表達**否定**的意思，通常會用「I don't think he/she/they will . . .」，而不會用「I think he/she/they won't . . .」這樣的句型。
· I don't think Vivian will like Sam.
我覺得薇薇安不會喜歡山姆。

Practice

1

利用題目提供的主詞，和動詞片語，以 will 分別造出疑問句、肯定句和否定句。

1. scientist　clone humans in 50 years
   - → Will scientists clone humans in 50 years?
   - → Scientists will clone humans in 50 years.
   - → Scientists won't clone humans in 50 years.

2. robots　become family members in 80 years
   - → _____
   - → _____
   - → _____

3. doctors　insert memory chips behind our ears
   - → _____
   - → _____
   - → _____

4. police officers　scan our brains for criminal thoughts
   - → _____
   - → _____
   - → _____

2

將題目提供的文字，分別以 I think、perhaps 和 I doubt 造句，並視情況使用「'll 的縮寫」形式。

1. I　live in another country
   - → I think I'll live in another country.
   - → Perhaps I'll live in another country.
   - → I doubt I'll live in another country.

2. my sister　learn how to drive
   - → _____
   - → _____
   - → _____

3. Jerry　marry somebody from another country
   - → _____
   - → _____
   - → _____

4. Tammy　not go abroad again
   - → _____
   - → _____
   - → _____

Unit **48**

Comparison Between "Will," "be Going to," and the Present Continuous

will、be going to 和現在進行式的比較

1 will 是「**突然決定的事件**」。

I've got a good idea. I'll buy her a baseball cap. ↳ 說話時刻做的決定
我想到一個好點子了，我要買個棒球帽給她。

Linda: The phone is ringing!
Nora: I'll get it.
琳達：電話響了！
諾拉：我來接。

2 be going to 則是「**事先決定好的事件**」。

What am I going to buy Mom for her birthday? ↳ 正在想這件事
我媽生日的時候，要買什麼禮物給她呢？

I'm going to drive to the sporting ↳ 事前已做的決定
goods store. 我打算開車去運動用品店。

I am going to buy a present for Mom's birthday. ↳ 事前已做的決定
我要去買我媽的生日禮物。

I'm going to make a ↳ 事先做好的決定
cup of coffee.
我要泡杯咖啡。

I'll make a cup of coffee. ↳ 臨時做的決定
我來泡杯咖啡吧。

She'll fall off the swivel chair. ↳ 認為可能會發生的事
她可能會從旋轉椅上跌下來。

She's going to fall off the swivel chair. ↳ 有徵兆已經可以預見
她快要從旋轉椅上跌下來了。

3 will 表示「**預測可能會發生的事情**」。

That guy looks like a thief. He'll steal your wallet if you're not careful.
那傢伙看起來像小偷。如果你不小心一點，他會偷走你的錢包。

Don't let Maggie know about this. She'll tell Mom.
不要跟瑪姬說，她可能會告訴媽媽。

4 be going to 表示「**從目前的狀況馬上可以預見的事情**」。

Watch out. He is going to steal your wallet.
小心，他打算要偷你的錢包。

Amy! You're going to crash into the tree!
艾美！你快撞到樹了。

5 現在**進行式**表示未來事件時，比較強調是一項「**安排**」；be going to 則強調「**意圖**」；will 則單純描述**未來事件**。

I'm flying to New York tomorrow morning. ↳ 機票已經買好
我明天早上就要飛去紐約。

I'm going to meet Mr. Simpson tomorrow night.
我明天晚上打算與辛普森先生會面。

I will be in Mexico next week.
我下星期人在墨西哥。

Practice

1

用括弧內提供的詞彙
改寫句子。

1. Will you go to the bookstore tomorrow? (be going to)

   → ....

2. Janet will help Cindy move in to her new house. (be going to)

   → ....

3. Are you going to play baseball this Saturday? (be + V-ing)

   → ....

4. He is going to cook dinner at 5:30. (will)

   → ....

5. She's going to fall into the water. (will)

   → ....

6. I will give him a call tonight. (be going to)

   → ....

7. When will you get up tomorrow morning? (be going to)

   → ....

8. I'll drive to Costco this afternoon. (be + V-ing)

   → ....

2

依提示用適當的動詞
形式完成句子。

1. She .... (leave) for Rome tomorrow. ▶ 安排

2. The ice cream .... (melt) if you don't finish it soon.

   ▶ 可能

3. I .... (quit) tomorrow! ▶ 臨時起意

4. I .... (quit) next month. I've been admitted to

   the university. ▶ 事先決定

5. I think I .... (eat) a sandwich. ▶ 臨時起意

6. Mr. Lee .... (have) dinner with Mr. Sun on Friday

   night. ▶ 安排

7. I .... (find) a good job, and I

   .... (make) a lot of money. ▶ 意圖

8. It .... (rain) tomorrow. ▶ 單純描述未來事件

Unit **49**
Review Test of Units 45–48
單元 45–48 總複習

1 根據題目提供的詞彙，以「現在進行式」完成肯定句，並將句子分別改寫為
「否定句」和「疑問句」。

→ Unit 1, 6 重點複習

1. I _____ (go) out for lunch tomorrow.

   → _____

   → _____

2. I _____ (plan) a birthday party for my grandmother.

   → _____

   → _____

3. She _____ (go) to take the dog for a walk after dinner.

   → _____

   → _____

4. Mike _____ (plan) to watch a baseball game later tonight.

   → _____

   → _____

5. Dr. Johnson _____ (meet) a patient at the clinic on Saturday.

   → _____

   → _____

6. Jack and Kim _____ (apply) for admission to a technical college.

   → _____

   → _____

7. I _____ (think) about having two kids after I get married.

   → _____

   → _____

8. Josh _____ (play) basketball this weekend.

   → _____

   → _____

9. My little brother _____ (plan) to sleep late on Sunday morning.

   → _____

   → _____

10. Father and I _____ (work) out at the gym on Sunday.

    → _____

    → _____

2 下列現在進行式的用法中，哪些是表示「正在進行的動作」？
哪些是表示「未來已經計畫好的事」？將表示正在進行的動作之句子寫上 C（continuous），
表示未來計畫之句子寫上 F（future）。
→ Unit 45 重點複習

.... 1. I'm eating out on Saturday night.

.... 2. Are you watching TV?

.... 3. Jennifer is making a doll now.

.... 4. Grandpa is watching a baseball game on TV at the moment.

.... 5. What are you doing now?

.... 6. I'm going downtown this Thursday.

.... 7. He's going on a date with Paula tonight.

.... 8. We're having dinner with the Smiths now.

3 將提示的主詞和動詞，以 be going to 的句型完成問句，並依提示以 be going to 的句型回答問題。
→ Unit 47 重點複習

1. What _are_ you _going to do_ (do) tomorrow night?
   I'm going to do some shopping tomorrow night. (do some shopping)

2. When _____ you _____ (leave)?
   _____ (at 9 a.m.)

3. _____ he _____ (call) her later?
   _____ (yes)

4. What _____ you _____ (say) when you see him?
   _____ (tell him the truth)

5. _____ they _____ (study) British Literature in college?
   _____ (Chinese Literature)

6. _____ your family _____ (have) a vacation in Hawaii?
   _____ (Guam)

125

4 自 **Solutions** 中選出適當的片語，用「I think I'll」的句型，寫出下列各項問題的解決方案。

→ Unit 47 重點複習

Problems

1. I'm tired. *I think I'll take a nap.*

2. It's too dark to see. _____

3. I just missed a phone call. _____

4. The grapes are ripe. _____

5. I received my phone bill. _____

6. It's my dad's birthday. _____

7. Emma is sick. _____

8. It's starting to rain. _____

Solutions

▲ buy him a gift

▲ take a nap

▲ bring my umbrella

▲ turn on a light

▲ check my voicemail

▲ visit her in the hospital

▲ pay it at 7-Eleven

▲ eat them right away

5 判斷下列句子的用法是否正確，正確的請打✓，錯誤的請改寫出正確的句子。
→ Unit 45–48 重點複習

1. Karl is working this weekend.
   ☐

2. I think it's raining soon.
   ☐

3. Harry is going to the grocery store later tonight.
   ☐

4. I'm sure you aren't getting called next week.
   ☐

5. Tina is going to write a screenplay.
   ☐

6. Is Laura going to working?
   ☐

7. I'll buy him a new bicycle.
   ☐

8. In the year 2100, people live on the moon.
   ☐

9. What are you do next week?
   ☐

6 選出正確的答案。
→ Unit 45–48 重點複習

1. Kelly : What are you going to do today?

   Sam : I think _____ my car.

   Ⓐ I'll clean   Ⓑ I'm going to clean   Ⓒ I'm cleaning

2. Don't touch that pot. _____.

   Ⓐ You'll get burned   Ⓑ You're going to get burned   Ⓒ You're getting burned

3. Tom : It's time to pick up Ellen.

   Larry : _____ right now.

   Ⓐ I'll leave   Ⓑ I'm going to leave   Ⓒ I will be leaving

4. I have an idea for Janie's graduation present. I think _____ a briefcase for her.

   Ⓐ I'll buy   Ⓑ I'm going to buy   Ⓒ I'm buying

7 將下列句子改寫為「否定句」和「疑問句」。

→ Unit 45–48 重點複習

1. I'll be watching the game on Saturday afternoon.
   → *I won't be watching the game on Saturday afternoon.*
   → *Will I be watching the game on Saturday afternoon?*

2. You're going to visit Grandma Moses tomorrow.
   →
   →

3. She's planning to be on vacation next week.
   →
   →

4. We're going to take a trip to New Zealand next month.
   →
   →

5. He'll send the tax forms soon.
   →
   →

6. It'll be cold all next week.
   →
   →

8 判斷下列句子的「未來形式」屬於何種用法，選出正確答案。

→ Unit 45–48 重點複習

.... 1. I'm thirsty. I'll get a drink.

Ⓐ Sudden decision   Ⓑ Predictable future   Ⓒ Intention

.... 2. It will be winter soon.

Ⓐ Simple future   Ⓑ Possibility   Ⓒ Plan in advance

.... 3. Be careful, or you will trip over a rock.

Ⓐ Sudden decision   Ⓑ Possibility   Ⓒ Simple future

.... 4. There're only ten seconds left. We're going to lose the game.

Ⓐ Simple future   Ⓑ Plan in advance   Ⓒ Predictable future

.... 5. I'm going to teach him a lesson.

Ⓐ Intention   Ⓑ Simple future   Ⓒ Sudden decision

.... 6. All my friends will come to my birthday party.

Ⓐ Predictable future   Ⓑ Simple future   Ⓒ Intention

.... 7. I'm going to buy a new car.

Ⓐ Simple future   Ⓑ Intention   Ⓒ Sudden decision

.... 8. I'm visiting Mrs. Jones this afternoon.

Ⓐ Fixed arrangement   Ⓑ Predictable future   Ⓒ Simple future

.... 9. Someone is knocking on the door. I'll see who it is.

Ⓐ Intention   Ⓑ Possibility   Ⓒ Sudden decision

.... 10. The sky is dark. It's going to rain.

Ⓐ Predictable future   Ⓑ Intention   Ⓒ Plan in advance

.... 11. I'm taking my dog to the vet on Saturday, so I can't go cycling with you.

Ⓐ Sudden decision   Ⓑ Simple future   Ⓒ Fixed arrangement

.... 12. We will probably go to Greece for our honeymoon.

Ⓐ Sudden decision   Ⓑ Possibility   Ⓒ Plan in advance

Progress Test

Part 1　名詞和冠詞

1 下列名詞是可數還是不可數？請在可數名詞的括弧內填上 C，不可數填上 U。

1. (　) adult
2. (　) crown
3. (　) mouse
4. (　) bicycle
5. (　) salt
6. (　) box
7. (　) grass
8. (　) honesty
9. (　) bread
10. (　) market

11. (　) child
12. (　) time
13. (　) soup
14. (　) number
15. (　) company
16. (　) chocolate
17. (　) juice
18. (　) money
19. (　) knowledge
20. (　) paper

2 請寫出下列單字的「複數名詞」。

1. giraffe
2. dish
3. ox
4. life
5. duck
6. church
7. size
8. eraser
9. goose
10. television
11. pencil
12. oasis
13. cherry
14. species
15. library

16. datum
17. sheep
18. fairy
19. deer
20. witch

3 請用 a、an 或 the 填空，完成句子。

1. He is _____ singer.
2. Her face looks like _____ moon.
3. Have you got _____ credit card?
4. Does this library have _____ on-line catalog?
5. Have you ever eaten _____ snake?
6. _____ elephant stepped on my toe.
7. Mommy, I want to buy _____ dog.
8. _____ apple a day keeps _____ doctor away.
9. Do we have to wait _____ hour?
10. Please pick up _____ dry cleaning.
11. I thought it was _____ honest apology.
12. _____ pears were ripe and juicy.
13. He said it was just _____ quick trip.
14. Bob says _____ party starts at 10:00.
15. It's _____ integrated digital watch, cell phone, and GPS locator.
16. It's _____ big store, but they didn't have it.
17. I'll meet you at _____ bookstore.
18. The vice president will arrive at _____ city hall in _____ minute.

4 請依據圖示，用適當的「量詞」填空，完成句子。

1. some _____ of mineral water

2. a _____ of chocolate

3. a _____ of toothpaste

4. two _____ of tea

5. a _____ of milk

6. a _____ of facial cream

7. a _____ of soda

8. a _____ of soup

9. a _____ of coconut milk

10. a _____ of cabbage

5 請圈選正確的答案。

1. There is heavy traffic / traffics during rush hour.

2. We need a truck to move the furniture / furnitures.

3. Don't run while holding scissor / scissors.

4. How many glasses of milk / milks should I pour?

5. If it's OK with you, I'd rather have tea / teas.

6. Did you realize this store sells many kinds of coffee / coffees?

6 若空格處需要 the，請填上；若不需要，請畫上「✕」。

1. Please put _____ gas in the car.

2. When will we arrive at _____ airport?

3. Buy me _____ coolest cell phone you can afford.

4. Let's meet at _____ 1:30 or 2 p.m.

5. When you get _____ stock certificate, put it in a safe place.

6. _____ report is due on Friday.

7. Are you going to the mall on _____ foot?

8. I went to Nina's apartment by _____ subway.

9. She's going to play _____ violin at the concert.

10. Living in _____ city is more convenient, but living in _____ country is healthier.

11. Jeffery loves _____ mathematics, but he doesn't like to study _____ chemistry.

12. Does your father play _____ golf on Sunday?

13. I need to get to _____ station before noon.

14. _____ dogs and _____ cats are friendly animals.

將錯誤的句子打✗，並寫出正確的句子。
若句子無誤，請在方框內打 ✓。

1. The Calvin is a cool little kid.

   | ✗ | *Calvin is a cool little kid.* |

2. Our vacation starts on the Friday, the
   January 20.

   | |

3. I am studying French, and I want to visit
   France.

   | |

4. The nearest airport is in the Canberra.

   | |

5. Museum of Modern Art in the New York is
   50 years old.

   | |

6. Great Wall of China is pretty amazing.

   | |

8
請將各名詞加上「's」、「'」或 of、of the。

1. Jane / hat
2. my grandparents / house
3. side / road
4. Beethoven / Fifth Symphony

5. products / price tags
6. ruins / ancient civilizations

9
下列句子是否需要加 the ？將錯誤的句子
打✗，並寫出正確的句子。若句子無誤，
請在方框內打 ✓。

1. Don't go to bed too late.

   | |

2. We are going by bus to avoid parking
   problems.

   | |

3. Are you watching the TV or doing the
   homework?

   | |

4. Do you want to go to the theater or the
   cinema?

   | |

5. Helen has decided to learn piano.

   | |

6. The closest star to us is Sun.

   | |

Part 2   代名詞

1 請用正確主詞代名詞（I、you、he、she、it、we、you 或 they）填空，完成句子。

1. My name is Paul. _____'m on the baseball team.

2. Johnny! Why are _____ hitting your sister?

3. There's food for everybody. _____ should get plates and help yourselves.

4. Back on the bus. _____'re leaving in five minutes.

5. Tom said _____'d be back sometime today.

6. I called your mother and father. _____ said no problem.

7. Alison is the fastest runner in our class, and _____ just won another race.

8. That soup is too spicy. I can't finish _____.

2 請圈選正確的答案。

1. Do you want to sit with me / my?

2. Who did you bring with your / you?

3. Harriet said that she knew him / his from school.

4. I have known hers / her for many years.

5. Come to think of it / its, she has changed her name.

6. That dog belongs to our / us. We'll clean up after it.

7. You / Your can all sit down now.

8. I'm not sitting here with you guys. I'm going over there and sit with their / them.

9. That new guy is on your team. This guy is on ours / our.

10. I can't find my / mine basketball anywhere.

11. I'll drive my car. You drive yours / your.

12. Is this cottage your / yours?

13. Is this hat yours? I see your name on it. It must be yours / your.

14. My tennis racquet has my name on it. That's not my / mine.

15. I heard your excuse. What is hers / her?

3 請用正確所有格形容詞（my、your、his、her、its、our 或 their）填空，完成句子。

1. I'm a sales representative. Here is _____ business card.

2. This is where my parents, wife, children, and I live. It's _____ house.

3. The cat is licking the fur on _____ paw.

4. They bought a second car, but there's no room in _____ garage.

5. Beth looks different. Did she get _____ hair permed?

6. He loves mirrors. He's always looking at _____ muscles.

7. Do you want _____ meals on separate checks?

4 請用 some 或 any 填空，完成句子。

1. Jack has .... laptops.
2. Larry doesn't have .... laptops.
3. Do you have .... laptops?
4. There were .... phone calls for Ian.
5. There weren't .... phone calls for you.
6. Were there .... phone calls for me?
7. Would you like .... chocolate milk?
8. Yes, ... chocolate milk is great.
9. Have you tried .... lobster sashimi?
10. No, I haven't eaten .... lobster sashimi before.
11. You should try .... It's tasty.
12. OK. I'll eat .... at the seafood restaurant.
13. Have you been to .... cold places recently?
14. No, I haven't been to .... cold places.
15. Do Sam and Ann have .... children?
16. Can I have .... bacon for breakfast?
17. I don't watch .... TV programs at night.
18. Did you see .... worms in Puffy's food?
19. Yes, I saw ...., so I threw it away.
20. May I take .... photos in the gallery?
21. No, you can't take .... photos in the gallery.
22. Shall I buy you .... food?
23. No, thanks. I don't want ....

5 請用 some、any 或 no 填空，完成下列對話。

Boy: Don't touch my tops. You can't play with ❶............... of them.

Girl: I can play with ❷................ Mommy said so.

Boy: You can play with the flashlight.

Girl: There are ❸............... batteries in the flashlight.

Boy: Do you have ❹............... candy?

Girl: I have ❺............... chocolate.

Boy: Give me ❻............... and I'll let you play with a top.

Girl: ❼............... chocolate unless you let me play with all your tops.

Boy: Can I have ❽............... of the chocolate candies?

Girl: ❾............... piece but this big one.

Boy: OK, but only ❿............... of the tops. Deal?

Girl: Deal.

6 請選出正確答案。

...... 1. How .... do those strawberries cost?
    Ⓐ much   Ⓑ many   Ⓒ a few

...... 2. Are there .... art museums in the city?
    Ⓐ much   Ⓑ a little   Ⓒ many

...... 3. I have .... paintings by Japanese artists.
    Ⓐ much   Ⓑ a lot of   Ⓒ a little

...... 4. Please give me .... salad.
    Ⓐ many   Ⓑ much   Ⓒ a little

...... 5. We need .... good men.
    Ⓐ a few   Ⓑ a little   Ⓒ much

...... 6. That's .... for now.
    Ⓐ much   Ⓑ enough   Ⓒ a lot of

7 請用 little、a little、few 或 a few 填空，完成句子。

1. I have _____ money with me. I can't dine out with you tonight.

2. I noticed _____ spelling errors in your paper, but not many.

3. She got _____ help from her brother during the most difficult time in her life, but she has no complaint about it.

4. _____ spice in the soup will make it taste better.

5. She invited _____ friends to her house last night.

6. There are only _____ oranges in the refrigerator. I can't make enough orange juice for everyone.

7. I need to make _____ calls now.

8. There's _____ buzzing noise. What's wrong with your phone line?

8 請在空格處填上 one 或 ones，並寫出它在該句中所指的物品。

1. I don't need another glass of juice. I already have _____ (= _____).

2. He needs to buy some new ties. The _____ (= _____) he has are too old.

3. I bought two pairs of shoes. Which _____ (= _____) do you like?

4. Do you still have that old jacket, the _____ (= _____) with the broken zipper?

9 請自下表選出適當的不定代名詞填空，完成句子。

somebody	anybody	nobody
everybody	someone	anyone
no one	everyone	something
anything	nothing	everything
somewhere	anywhere	nowhere
everywhere		

1. I'm the only person here. _____ else has gone home.

2. You don't have a date, do you? I bet you haven't asked _____.

3. It looks as if you might be having a little trouble. Is there _____ wrong?

4. The phone call is for you. It's _____ from your office.

5. No, you can't drink any alcohol. We'll have _____ to drink when we get home.

6. That is a local flower. It grows here and _____ else.

7. I haven't said a thing. _____ has asked me about it.

8. Now you can make a cell phone call _____ in the world.

9. I'm hungry. I had _____ to eat all day.

10 請用 this、that、these 或 those 填空，完成句子。

1. Let's ask _____ guy over there.

2. Let's ask _____ child standing right next to you.

3. Let's ask _____ policemen right here.

4. Let's ask _____ man way over there by the shoe store.

5. Let's ask _____ cab drivers on the opposite side of the street.

11 請自下表選出正確的「反身代名詞」填空，完成句子。

myself	yourself	himself	herself
itself	ourselves	yourselves	
themselves			

1. He is looking at _____ in the mirror.

2. She never gives _____ a break.

3. If we don't do it _____, it will never be finished.

4. They moved their things _____ without the help of a moving company.

5. She always says, "I can do it _____," but then she never gets things done.

6. There isn't enough time for you to cook dinner _____ .

1 請用 am、is 或 are 填空，完成下列段落。

I **❶**_____ a traveling salesman. Today my sales meeting **❷**_____ in Townville. Tomorrow my presentation **❸**_____ in Smallville. I **❹**_____ always busy. I **❺**_____ an employee of Toothbrush Inc. We **❻**_____ the biggest toothbrush company in the world. My job title **❼**_____ Senior Sales Manager, but there **❽**_____ no people for me to manage. It **❾**_____ just me with my toothbrush samples. I have to visit two more stores, then I **❿**_____ done for the day. That **⓫**_____ my life.

2 請用 there is、there are、is there、are there、it is 或 they are 填空，完成句子。

Man: Let's go visit my Uncle Fred on his farm in Ruralville.

Woman: **❶**_____ anything interesting to do in Ruralville?

Man: **❷**_____ lots of interesting things to do.

Woman: Tell me about all those interesting things in Ruralville.

Man: Uhhh? You can enjoy nature. **❸**_____ a quiet place.

Woman: **❹**_____ many people?

Man: No, but **❺**_____ a very nice place.

Woman: So, **❻**_____ nothing interesting to do.

Man: Well . . . no.

Woman: You go visit the cows and the corn. I'm staying right here.

3 請用 **have got** 的正確形式填空完成句子。
（注意：**have / has got**，主要用於英式英文。）

1. I _____ a dog and a cat.

2. I _____ (not) any fish.

3. Tim: _____ you _____ any pets?
   Kim: Yes, I _____.

4. They _____ two kids, but they
   _____ (not) any pets.

4 請將括弧內的動詞以「簡單現在式」填空，
完成句子。

1. I _____ (work) downtown in the city.

2. I _____ (take) the train to get to my
   office.

3. My wife _____ (commute) to work
   by bus.

4. How _____ you _____ (get) to
   your work?

5. I _____ (not drive) .
   I _____ (not know) how.

6. _____ you _____ (go) shopping at
   the new mall?

7. It _____ (take) me 20 minutes to
   commute to work.

5 請將括弧內的動詞以「現在進行式」填空，
完成句子。

1. What _____ you _____ (do) right
   now?

2. The phone in the kitchen _____
   (ring) .

3. I _____ not _____ (cook)
   dinner tonight.

4. My boss _____ (look) for
   someone to come in and provide some
   technical leadership.

5. _____ you _____ (work) now?

6. I _____ (plan) to take some
   days off.

6 選出正確的答案。

_____ 1. Sometimes I _____ at this mini-mart.
   Ⓐ am shopping   Ⓑ shop   Ⓒ shops

_____ 2. I usually _____ a cup of coffee at this
   café.
   Ⓐ am buying   Ⓑ buy   Ⓒ buys

_____ 3. I _____ the newspaper right now.
   Ⓐ read   Ⓑ reads   Ⓒ am reading

_____ 4. I always _____ the headlines before I
   read a newspaper.
   Ⓐ checks   Ⓑ am checking   Ⓒ check

_____ 5. He _____ the newspaper every day at
   lunch.
   Ⓐ reads   Ⓑ read   Ⓒ is reading

_____ 6. He _____ out an article from the
   newspaper.
   Ⓐ cut   Ⓑ cuts   Ⓒ is cutting

_____ 7. Jim _____ tea and reads the newspaper
   every morning.
   Ⓐ drink   Ⓑ drinks   Ⓒ is drinking

_____ 8. Ann: Are you reading a novel now?
   Bob: I _____.
   Ⓐ do   Ⓑ am   Ⓒ is

_____ 9. Kelly: Do you like to read novels on
   Sundays?
   Jimmy: I _____.
   Ⓐ do   Ⓑ is   Ⓒ am

將錯誤的句子打✗，並寫出正確的句子。
若句子無誤，請在方框內打 ✓。

1. I am wanting something to eat.

   ☐ ....

2. I am loving that dress you are wearing.

   ☐ ....

3. She has all sorts of new clothes.

   ☐ ....

4. I am thinking you are right about Jim.

   ☐ ....

5. Irene is having lunch now.

   ☐ ....

6. I was seeing some new shopping bags in
   your closet.

   ☐ ....
   ....

⟫⟫⟫ Part 4 過去時態

1 請用 be 動詞的過去式填空，完成句子。

1. Pete: .... Linda and Randy on
   vacation last month?

   Greg: Yes, they ....

2. .... that movie on TV last night?
   No, it ....

3. Tony: .... she attractive in her new
   dress yesterday?

   Randy: Yes, she ....

4. Jason: .... they at the party last night?
   Mia: No, they ....

2 請用「過去簡單式」填空，完成對話。

Dad: ❶............ you ❷............ (go) to meet
     your girlfriend's parents?

Son: I ❸............ (meet) them last Sunday.

Dad: What ❹............ (happen) ?

Son: We ❺............ (eat) dinner and
     ❻............ (talk) .

Dad: What else ❼............ you ❽............ (do) ?

Son: We just ❾............ (stay) at their
     house.

Dad: It sounds like an adult dinner party.

Son: Yes, her parents ❿............ (behave)
     themselves very well.

Dad: I ⓫............ (mean) you.

Son: I ⓬............ (be) well behaved, too.

3 請用「過去簡單式」與「過去進行式」填空，
完成這篇故事。

I ❶............ (stand) on Market Street
waiting for my bus, and a guy in a black jacket
❷............ (sit) on a bench across the
street waiting for his bus. A pizza delivery
woman ❸............ (pull up) near the guy
in the black jacket. The pizza woman
❹............ (grab) one of the pizzas out
of her car and ran into a nearby building. She
had left her car with the motor running in the "No
Parking" zone where the bus usually stops.
I ❺............ (notice) the guy across the
street stand up. He ❻............
(look) at the pizza woman's car. The guy
❼............ (start) walking around the
pizza car. I shouted at him as he
❽............ (open) the car door, got in,
and drove away. He had stolen the car and a
stack of six pizzas. The pizza woman

⑨ _____ (begin) to cry when she
⑩ _____ (discover) that her car and
pizzas were gone.

4 請將括弧內的動詞以「現在完成式」填空，
完成句子。

1. Mr. Keller _____ (be) a lawyer
   since 1984.
2. _____ you ever _____
   (attend) a wedding on the top of a
   mountain?
3. Julie _____ (have) a perm
   and highlighting done to her hair.
4. Tim _____ (leave) and I hope
   he never returns.
5. Rocky _____ (be) out all night
   and has not returned yet.

5 請圈選正確的答案。

1. Who opened / has opened the boxes
   before I arrived?
2. I had / have had my present car for three
   years.
3. Have you been / Did you go to Australia?
4. Have you been / Did you go to Café
   Budapest last night?

>>> **Part 5** 未來時態

1 將括號內的動詞以「現在進行式」填空，
完成下列表示未來意義的句子。

Dan: ❶_____ you ❷_____ (see) the
doctor tomorrow?

Ann: No, I ❸_____ (see) the
doctor this afternoon.

Dan: I ❹_____ (go) to the concert
on Saturday. ❺_____ you
❻_____ (come) with me?

Ann: I wish I could, but I
❼_____ (meet) an
important client from Miami.

Dan: ❽_____ you ❾_____
(take) any trips in March?

Ann: I ❿_____ (visit) some
customers in Australia and New Zealand.

2 將括弧內的動詞以 be going to 的句型填
空，完成下列表示未來意義的句子。

1. I am tired. I _____
   (sleep) .
2. When _____ you _____
   (visit) your friends in Hong Kong?
3. _____ you _____ (quit)
   your job after the company gives out
   bonuses?
4. Why _____ you _____
   (move) to Japan?
5. _____ you _____ (live) with
   your parents?

3 將括弧內的動詞搭配 will 或 won't 填空，
完成下列表示未來意義的句子。

1. He ＿＿＿＿＿＿＿＿＿＿ (wonder) why I
   dumped him.

2. No way! I ＿＿＿＿＿＿＿＿＿ (date) that
   jerk again.

3. He ＿＿＿＿＿＿＿＿＿ (send) me some
   flowers and little gifts.

4. I ＿＿＿＿＿＿＿＿ (screen) his calls and
   refuse to answer.

5. I ＿＿＿＿＿＿＿＿ (respond) no matter
   what he does.

Let's See Grammar
彩圖初級英文文法 Basic 1 三版

作　　　者	Alex Rath Ph.D.
審　　　訂	Dennis Le Boeuf & Liming Jing
譯　　　者	謝右／丁宥榆
校　　　對	歐寶妮
編　　　輯	賴祖兒／丁宥榆／陸葵珍
主　　　編	丁宥暄
內 文 設 計	洪伊珊／林書玉
封 面 設 計	林書玉
圖 片 協 力	周演音
製 程 管 理	洪巧玲
出 版 者	寂天文化事業股份有限公司
發 行 人	黃朝萍
電　　　話	+886-(0)2-2365-9739
傳　　　真	+886-(0)2-2365-9835
網　　　址	www.icosmos.com.tw
讀 者 服 務	onlineservice@icosmos.com.tw
出 版 日 期	2022 年 9 月 三版再刷（0302）

國家圖書館出版品預行編目 (CIP) 資料

Let's See Grammar：彩圖初級英文文法 Basic / Alex
Rath 著 . -- 三版 . -- [臺北市]：寂天文化事業股份有限
公司 , 2021.02
面；　公分
ISBN 978-986-318-973-2　（第 1 冊：菊 8K 平裝）
ISBN 978-986-318-974-9　（第 2 冊：菊 8K 平裝）
1. 英語　2. 語法
805.16　　　　　　　　　　　　　　110000944